Wiskalo Chookalo

THE HAUNTING OF UPPSALA, WISCONSIN

Edward S. Louis

Wiskalo Chookalo
The Haunting of Uppsala, Wisconsin

Authored by Edward S. Louis
Edited by Mary Paplham

Published by Peregrino Press
De Pere, WI
www.peregrino.press

Interior design by Euan Monaghan
Cover design by Travis J. Vanden Heuvel
Cover photo © Peregrino Press. ALL RIGHTS RESERVED

Publisher's note:
This story, including names, characters, places, and incidents, is a work of imaginative fiction. Any chance resemblance to actual persons, locations, or events is purely coincidental. The author alone bears responsibility for any remaining errors in the text, which are wholly unintentional.

ISBN (hardcover): 978-1-949042-90-0
ISBN (paperback): 978-1-949042-07-8
This title is also available in electronic and audiobook formats.

PUBLISHER'S CATALOGING-IN-PUBLICATION DATA
Louis, Edward S.
Wiskalo Chookalo / Edward S. Louis
1st edition. De Pere, WI: Peregrino Press, c2018.

Printed in the United States of America
10 9 8 7 6 5 4 3 2 1

**For Henry and Mary Lou
and for Bev**

Nearly any artistic or intellectual project requires help if its author hopes to find it a place in the world. I offer my sincere appreciation and thanks to Beverly Green, who believed in this book from first draft to print, to Bob Boyer and Scott Winkler, who encouraged me and led me to Travis and Peregrino, to Travis Vanden Heuvel for finding the spirituality in this text and taking on the project, to Tracy Williams and Norbert Hill for help with my questions on Oneida language and history, to Mary Paplham for another instance of quick, attentive, and professional editing, and to Kristy for tolerating all my tales of woe as *Wiskalo Chookalo* made its fraught and circuitous way to publication.

WHAT OTHERS ARE SAYING ABOUT *WISKALO CHOOKALO*:

A World War II veteran stumbles upon a small 1930's Midwest town beset by a mysterious, flesh-eating earth spirit. As psychic distress compounds economic woe, only a blend of Native American wisdom and medieval Icelandic tactic can free the region of the night-prowling menace. E. S. Louis's impressive grasp of folklore, across continents, and his compassionate depiction of a veteran of the Great War piecing together a life during the Great Depression combine to make this no ordinary ghost story.

Professor Dominique Battles
Author of *Cultural Difference and Material Culture in Middle English Romance* and *The Medieval Tradition of Thebes*

Beowulf meets *The Exorcist*. The Grendel which Edward Louis's wandering Depression-era hero confronts is part earth-spirit, part emanation of the hatreds and injustices soaked into the soil, but at the same time entirely physical, a man-eater holding a township in terror and paralysis. This is folk-tale viewed through a stern and critical prism, the cheap thrills and reflexes of video-game heroics understood and rebutted. A fresh and notable addition to the literature of the weird.

Professor Tom Shippey
Author of *J.R.R. Tolkien: Author of the Century* and *The Road to Middle-earth*

Wiskalo Chookalo has all the vivid detail of a good ghost story: its central character comes with a supernatural calling card that stays with you. Perhaps more remarkably in a work of this size, the story's human characters are unusually authentic, a quality that emerges in rich dialogue and relationships of real emotional depth.

Tyler Cloherty
Acquisitions Editor, Medieval Institute Pub. and ARC Humanities Press

Edward Louis has written a ripping good ghost story in *Wiskalo Chookalo*. He presents an imaginative narrative that is all the more enjoyable for its rich cultural and historical context. But like all classic ghost tales, Louis' story is ultimately about good and evil—and us.

Thomas Kunkel
Author of *Man in Profile, Joseph Mitchell of The New Yorker*

Wiskalo Chookalo will have readers smiling, questioning, and reflecting, sometimes in rapid succession—or all at once. They will enjoy listening to the epic character-narrator by the name of Hank Peck. They follow his adventures from the battlefields of World War One France to the coal mines of West Virginia and finally to Central Wisconsin around 1933 during the Great Depression. He arrives by train, as a gentleman hobo, at a small Wisconsin town that seems to be possessed by a ghost. With the help of an adept Oneida seer, her war-veteran brother, and a stray dog, Hank attempts to help the reluctant townspeople face their ghost. The ghost and the array of characters are Dickens; the setting is Steinbeck. *Wiskalo Chookalo* is a rare gem.

Robert H. Boyer
Author of *The Magic Necklace of Al-Andalus*

RIGHT OUT OF THE EARTH

Two of the McBride brothers, Miles and Jake, stood in the middle of the road.

The third, Arvin, had remained back in the West Virginia mountains. He had troubles of his own, but his brothers wished he had come with them. He was bigger than they were and braver than they were, and back then they believed safety came in numbers.

They had only the two of them on that dark, frosty evening hidden among the trees just a piece south of Uppsala, Wisconsin, plus their dog, Buck, a big mixed-breed, white with black markings. The month was November, and the year was 1876.

Miles had his Winchester loaded and ready. Jake had a torch in his hand and a Colt revolver holstered at his side. His hand was shaking, causing the torchlight to cast grotesque shadows among the trees.

"Try to stay still, Jake. They say it feeds on fear. Can smell it a mile away."

"I'm no scareder than you are, Miles. I can hear your bones rattling."

An overwhelming feeling of dread nearly made them both lie down in the road. They were too afraid to run or to pray.

"We got to get this done, Miles," Jake said. "We can't have it around anymore."

"It's the Indians' fault," Miles said. "They cursed us with it."

"It isn't the Indians' fault," Jake replied.

"Then it's the Swedes' fault. They brought it with them."

"Not the Swedes' fault, either, Miles. It came because of us, because of what we did. Or maybe it was always here, waiting."

"I hope we don't have to wait long," Miles said. "I hate waiting. It's freezing out here. Can't believe it hasn't snowed yet."

Jake, on the other hand, could wait. He could wait a hundred years, a thousand years, for what they had come out to do. He could wait forever. But he didn't tell his brother that.

"If it comes, don't look straight at it: don't look it in the eyes," Miles warned. "It will freeze you in your tracks. That's what happened to Old McGrath. He never got off a shot. His son told me. He said . . ."

"I know what he said."

Before they realized it, the dusk had turned to dark, the deep dark of early winter that comes too soon and goes too late.

Time passed. It may have been an hour.

Miles' teeth were chattering.

"Sshhh: look at Buck."

"Big old Buck—bravest dog I ever seen," whispered Miles.

About fifty yards ahead of them, down in the middle of the path, Buck sat waiting, too. Then he recoiled and shivered from the ground up to the tip of his ears. His fur stood straight up on his back, his nose pointed toward the sky, and his howl pierced the dusk and echoed in the trees. The brothers, hunters since they were children growing up in the Appalachian Mountains, had never heard such a sound like that howl. Backing up, Buck nearly fell into the pit the brothers had dug and carefully covered in the road. He stopped, dropped to the ground, and then began to back up again, snarling.

Just in front of Buck a blue-white light began to rise up from the ground like smoke.

Then Buck began to leap repeatedly in the air, as if he were dancing with flames licking out of a roaring campfire.

"Zig, Buck, zig!" Jake called out. But not in time: an enormous hand with claws like bayonets pushed out of that white light and swept Buck up out of the road and into the trees. The dog wailed and disappeared into the shadows.

"It's real!" Jake hissed. "It's real. It's coming up right out of the earth! The ghost! God help us!"

The fey light congealed into a shape, tall, solid, bright white, and menacing. A low growl came from its center, and the growl rose into a wail that shook the trees like a high wind. It echoed through the air above them. The stars themselves fell into shadow, and the cold, thin moon disappeared behind a cloud.

"W a a a a A A A A A A y e e e o o o o o o o o O O W W ! Woo-woo-woowwoooOOOOOOyyaaAAHH!"

Twice as fast as the fastest horse could run, the shape made right for them.

And just as suddenly it fell.

"The pit!" Miles screamed. "The pit! It worked! Hurry!"

Miles pulled up his stiff, frozen feet, took a few steps forward, and heaved his torch into the pit.

A scream—a scream of pain or anger or both. The ghost screamed with the malice of anger and hatred as old as time. A great flame burst out of the pit as if a bomb had gone off in it.

The fire brought pain, but it did not consume its victim—only made it angrier.

Then over the top of the pit came two long hands with razor-sharp claws. They curled to gather force, and they pulled. The great blue-white shape leaped out of the pit and howled again its piercing, grinding, paralyzing, schizophrenic wail.

Miles got off several shots from his Winchester, and Jake pulled his handgun, but before he could shoot, he realized that his brother was running as fast as he could back toward town. Jake tried to shoot behind him as he ran. The bullets did nothing, whether they hit or not.

With a last glance back Jake saw Buck tearing out of the trees and right for the shape. Brave dog indeed!

The ghost, which had before been bathed in its own light, hissed with fire, a ruthless tar-fire from the pit into which it had fallen. The flames raged, but they did not consume.

W U U U U U U H H H H H ! W U H ! Wooo OOOO OOOOOOOAAAAAHHHH! WAAAAA!

Before Buck could jump at it, the light turned its eyes on the poor dog. Buck fell to the ground whimpering, the last of the fight drained out of him.

But in those few seconds the brothers, driven by utter fear, made headway toward town.

The ghost, ghoul, or creature as may be, with flames rising and dancing from it, pursued them with a ferocity unknown to men or beasts.

Miles dashed into the open door of his barn, slammed and barred it. Jake leaped through the open door of his house, skidded to stop, and went back and slammed the door shut.

A second later his front door burst in.

Someone from up the road who had dared to peek outside said that the house caught fire and burned to cinders in minutes. Neither Jake nor his two older sons, who were waiting there for him armed with shotguns of their own, were ever seen or heard from again. His wife and youngest son survived: Jake had sent them to stay with cousins on the other side of town.

Some of the townsfolk who had tried to keep the fire from spreading found Miles face-down, hiding in the barn the next morning. He was alive, but he had gone mad.

The people of Uppsala say that a ghost dog, a large mutt, white with black markings, sometimes appears in the woods and on the lanes or paths that lead to town, usually in November. They say that it howls out warnings to those passing by, but no one stays long to listen: the howling terrifies them.

Of the ghost they say little if anything, other than it will appear at night, and no one in that town will go out in the dark.

They believe that even to speak of it will bring it right back out of the ground again.

Three homes besides the McBrides' burned down that night, though the other families escaped. People later rebuilt those three, but no one ever tried to rebuild the house of Jake McBride that stood beside his brother's on the east lane into town.

That happened years before our story, but the people of Uppsala remembered it. They didn't like to speak of it, but they remembered. And they never did welcome strangers.

On occasion the ghost will reappear, always at night, to the imprudent resident or the unwary traveler. Some have heard it wail. A few have seen it. No one, the locals used to say, has looked it in the eye.

A PROLOGUE, A PROLEPSIS

In the early 1990's I went to see a man about a ghost.

Telling his story seemed to please the old man.

He gave me permission to tell it or write it, as long as I stuck to the facts as he told them.

He wasn't as hard to find as I expected, nor as reticent: he spoke readily.

Everyone I'd asked when I first got to town knew him. No one thought he'd talk with me, though they all said he was nice enough. He just didn't like to talk to strangers anymore. But as soon as I met him, we hit it off. He must have been able to see that I had an honest interest in his story and in him.

I got there early in the afternoon on a fall-ish Saturday, and the air was a little cool. He was sitting on the porch of an old farmhouse. I'd walked out from town—not very far—because Clare, the lady I spoke to at the diner, told me he didn't like cars. The drive to Green Lake, not far from his home, wouldn't take long, and I had started early. The day before, I'd stopped in Madison first to visit my old Folklore professor. By the time I got to Green Lake, I was tired of driving and didn't mind stretching my legs. A cool September breeze just ruffled the trees that lined the small road to his house.

He had a blanket over his legs, but when I waved to him, he took it off and stood up nimbly and waved a welcome.

"You the fella Clare told me about?" I saw he had a phone sitting next to his chair on the porch. It looked like a first generation mobile phone, and from what I'd heard of him, that phone surprised me even more than his obvious vitality. He also had a nice-sized boombox sitting by the door, and it was playing a late-season Brewers' game. He had to be in his mid-90s, but he looked plenty spry. I hadn't expected that he would like technology—my own prejudice. Clare had obviously called to announce me, probably so he could go inside and close the door if he didn't want to see me.

"Yes. Would you mind talking for a bit?"

He motioned me up, took off the Fedora that sat a-tilt over his forehead, and held out his hand. I took it, and he still had a grip that a blacksmith would have envied. "Hank Peck," he said.

"Pleased to meet you, Mr. Peck."

"There's another chair in the corner by the window. Pull it over. What's in the bag?"

Clare, the proprietor of the only diner in town, had again come through for me. She'd told me he liked coffee with double cream and sugar. I'd brought two big cups.

"Coffee?" I asked.

"Double cream and sugar?"

"You bet."

He laughed, nodded, and took one. "Clare knows me too well. Not many folks do." He took a long, slow sip and sighed.

He wasn't tall, maybe five foot eight or nine, though he may have been a bit taller when he was younger. His forearms were still broad, round, and muscular, his shoulders square, and his face nearly free of wrinkles, though he had a few small scars on his chin and around his eyes. His hair, still thick, was an iron gray with a few streaks of dark brown still in it. His eyes were sky blue, clear and aware—think Peter O'Toole, but with a strength that could knock down a grown man if he looked there too hard. Yet the eyes, clear as they were, looked tired, like those of a person who has worked too hard and needs a good rest. He shifted the hat to the back of his head and sat down.

I gave my name, and he nodded.

"I don't care much for small talk. Hope you don't mind," he said. It wasn't an apology, but a simple statement of fact. "I hear you're interested in what happened over in Uppsala, 'bout an hour from here, back in the thirties."

14

"Professor Akembe at the University told me a little about it, but he's heard only rumors. Said I should talk with you in person, if you were still living."

He laughed. "Yes, still living, though that's hard to believe with all I been through. I think I got a letter from him, Akembe, once, but it's not the kind of story you tell in a letter. Told him he was welcome to come up and hear it if he liked. Guess he sent you. Seems like a good man. African?"

"Yes, he's a very good man. Taught me most of what I know. Kenyan. He's studied folklore and folktales all over the world, and probably lived some of his own."

"You look too old to be a student of his. You a professor, too?"

"Yes. I teach at a small school upstate."

"Like your work?"

I took a big drink of coffee and looked into those sky-blue eyes. I saw a steady character with confidence, no pretense, and no guile. "I love my work."

"Good. I like to hear a man say that that he's fond of his work. Or a woman. Makes no difference these days, I guess. My only daughter went to California to learn how to make movies, and she's some kind of producer there now. And good for her, I say. You have to understand that I come from a different time. You like your students? They any good?"

"Yes, I like them—like them a lot. Some do really well. Some don't try as hard as you'd like, but that's their own business."

"Right. You teach folktales or history?" he asked. Beside him on his right sat a small table with a book and what looked like a pair of simple reading glasses on top. The book was a history of World War I.

"I don't get to teach folklore so much, but I write about it. Especially at a small school you have to teach what they need you to teach. So I teach anthropology and mythology mostly, sometimes Greek if anyone's interested."

"Good. Do you know the difference between what's a story and what really happened?"

I had to try hard not to laugh because I could tell that he meant it, and I understood. "Does anyone?" I asked.

Then he laughed again, this time a firm, deep laugh that made his chest shake. "Right you are, son. But if I'm going to tell you this story, I'm going to tell you the truth, not a folktale, though it may sound to you like one."

"Fine by me. I'm here to listen."

"Well, I hope you've got a while, because if I'm going to tell it, I'm going to tell it all. Haven't ever done that, tell all of it. But I don't have a lot longer to live now, and somebody should know it, all of it, at least all that one man can tell. You comfortable there?"

The chair wasn't particularly comfortable, but I nodded anyway. I was eager to listen to Hank Peck's story of Wiskalo Chookalo. Dr. Akembe had told me that the little he knew of it made his hair stand on end, and he's one of the bravest human beings I've ever known.

"Do you mind if I record it?"

"Hmmm, don't know—well, why not? You should get it down on paper, too, in case your recorder doesn't work. That what's filling up the rest of your bag?"

I took out a small recorder and my tablet and pen.

"Wait a minute," he said.

Still quick to his feet, he went inside and returned almost immediately with a pillow.

"Put that on your chair. You're not really comfortable, but I know you were trying to be polite. That will help. Right: that's better. Start your recorder any time you'd like."

I used the plug that was by his front door to save the batteries. "How's the book you're reading?" I asked.

"Pretty good: she got nearly everything right, at least all of it that I can remember."

"Ready? Will you tell me a little about yourself first? I don't want to pry, but that may help me work up the story later."

"That seems reasonable enough. What would you like to know?"

"Whatever has a bearing on the story, or whatever you'd like to tell. Where do you come from? You're not a Wisconsin native."

"How'd you know?"

"Accent's not the same. Somewhere around Pittsburgh?"

16

"You got it! Small town in Ohio maybe fifty miles from Pittsburgh. Born January 1, 1900. My father was an old-time blacksmith. Not a tall man, but he had forearms as thick as footballs and shoulders like bowling balls, hands as broad as a shovel. Could barely fit a size sixteen ring on his little finger. His name wasn't originally Peck. His father changed it when they came over from Poland. He never told me exactly what it was, though I was once heard someone call him *Pecarowicz* or something like that. Never met any of his family to get that name straight. He was a good man and a serious Catholic and knew the Latin Mass by heart.

"My mother was an Irish lass, first generation American. She had the biggest, bluest eyes you've ever seen, and more energy than you'd expect from someone who was underfed her whole life. She took in washing to make extra money, and she could fix anything broken that the neighbors brought over—she had an amazing knack for that, fixing gadgets she'd never even seen before. The two of them took me to Mass every Sunday from the time I can first remember anything, and they made sure I prayed every night. And I kept praying until I got back from the War—couldn't do it so much after that, though it's come in useful a couple times since.

"Dad died when I was seven: they said his forge exploded. Nothing left of his body but burnt tar and ash. When we heard, my mother ran right over, and I went behind as fast as I could. It broke her heart: she loved that man. We tried to get along together for a couple years, but she couldn't make enough money. I tried doing little jobs for people, washing windows, picking apples, painting, that sort of thing, but they'd as like not forget to pay me for them. Mother sent me to Texas to live with her brother: he had a steady income working in the oil fields. She got me a train ticket and gave me a letter to give to my uncle when I got there. The train took me most of the way, and I hitched the rest on wagons and a couple of Ford's first cars, Model A's. For the first two years she wrote to me every week, and I'd write back in my scratchy little hand as best I could.

"My uncle wasn't the kindest man God ever made. When he saw the letter my mother had sent, he tore it up and dropped the shreds where he

17

stood. I picked them up and pieced them back together myself. The letter asked him to take care of me for a time and be sure I went to school.

"Now I'm not complaining. He gave me a roof over my head and food such as anybody got, but I had to work for all of it, cleaning up for him and the other men who lived in the shacks outside the oil fields. But there was no talk of schooling. By the time I was ten I was working in the fields myself, hauling tools and doing whatever odd jobs the men ordered me to do. They'd give me a few odd coins, and I'd use them to buy books that some of the men had read already and didn't want anymore. I taught myself to read with them and cast-off newspapers, and I learned arithmetic from buying things the men would send me for—if I'd got the change wrong, they'd have beaten me but good.

"The workers came from all over. My father had spoken English at work, but he spoke Polish to me at home. Mother had good English, but she'd use some Irish Gaelic now and then, too. In the Texas fields I heard men speaking French, Spanish, and German, and I picked up what I could of that: kids can learn a lot if adults let them. I never found any other Catholics. Most of the men who had any religion were Baptists or Methodists. On Sundays I'd find a place to hide and say my rosary by myself.

"I also learned how to stay out of people's way. They were a pretty mean bunch down there in Texas. The oil men would set a couple boys to fighting just to amuse themselves, and they'd bet on who'd win. They didn't mind matching a bigger boy against a little one: they seemed to enjoy watching the blood fly. I had my first scraps there, but tried to keep out of them. I was still a good Catholic, but I found that if someone came after me, something angry would come over me, and I couldn't stop until I'd knocked him down and out or he'd done the same to me. Uncle never said anything about the fighting one way or the other. In fact, I don't think he said two whole sentences to me in all the time I was there.

"As you can imagine, I got out of Texas as soon as I could. I had to hide my pennies from my uncle, and when I was thirteen, I just left and hitched back up north. Had a hankering to see New York. I got short-term jobs working on the docks on the East Coast. The workers there weren't so different from the oil-field men in Texas, just a little better organized. They'd get the teenaged boys into bare-knuckle brawling matches, ring and all. That was the only time I was glad for my time in Texas. The matches were tough, too tough for many of us, but I made enough extra money at them to pay my way to the city and get a real hotel room for a day. Was lucky I kept all my teeth. And all that scrapping had knocked any normal fear right out of me.

"Finally worked my way to the city when I was sixteen. It was a noisy, dirty, crowded mess, and I hated it from first sight. Caught a train to Philadelphia, then made my way through southern Pennsylvania working on farms—I'd just bunk down wherever the farm families would let me. Learned a lot about farm animals and a little about fishing and hunting—I'd trap rabbits for the meat and to sell the pelts. Never squirrels, though: I always kind of liked them. Don't know why. I'd let them go if I found them in a trap. I could have lived happily on a farm if that had been my lot, but I'd have wanted one of my own, and earlier in my life I never had enough money for that. I did get a few days here and there to go to school when there wasn't anything to do on the farms. Nothing much, just a few days here and there, but I got a little math, corrected my reading and writing mistakes, and learned some geography and rather better French.

"I wrote letters to my mother every week. Don't know if she got them, but writing made me feel better. I wasn't mad about her sending me off, but I wanted to get home with something to show for myself so she wouldn't think I'd done wrong by leaving my uncle.

"That was just before America got itself into the Great War. We heard a lot about it and read about it in the newspapers. When it looked like the U.S. would get in, a number of the farm boys where I was didn't want to go because of their religious commitments. I don't blame them for that. The others, the less well off, anyway, couldn't wait to sign up, so they got someone to drive them up to Canada. I went with them: saw the army as a way to make something of myself. Told the recruiters I was eighteen even though I was barely seventeen, and they either believed me or didn't care. I suspect that, given some of the grim business I'd already been through, one look at my face convinced them.

19

"Got to France in 1917 and saw action there and in Belgium. When the Americans got over there, my Canadian outfit got me re-assigned to the 3rd U.S. Infantry. I could talk about those days, but that's not what you came to hear. I can tell you, though, that I was at Verdun watching Eddie Rickenbacker fly over the field in his SPAD XIII at 10:45 in the morning of November 11, 1918, and later that day I saw for myself the bullet holes in the fuselage of his plane.

"A lot of boys—on both sides—went to that war hoping it would make men out of them. Mostly it just made dead boys out of them. Don't ask me if I killed anyone. People always ask that, except veterans—they never do. I took orders, shot my Springfield, and learned how to use a knife, but I also learned to treat wounds, improved my French and German, and got good with maps. They turned a pretty tough teenage boy into a piece of unyielding leather. I'm just glad I never got gassed.

"At the end of the war I met a French girl who was returning to her bombed-out village: some of us were trying to help the natives get re-settled. She was beautiful, but poverty and the war had reduced her to almost nothing. I convinced myself I could nurse her back to health. We got married, though we were just two homeless kids. She died in the flu epidemic of 1918.

"When I got back to the U.S., I went as quickly as I could to try to find my mother. Some folks in our hometown remembered her, and someone thought she'd moved up around Canton, Ohio, during the War. After about two months I found an aunt there; she had a letter that my mother had written for me. My aunt took me to my mother's grave.

"She was a good woman, my aunt, a lot like my mother and not at all like her brother. She moved to Duluth, Minnesota, with her second husband, and she was the reason I was in Wisconsin to begin with: I was on my way to Duluth to stay with her. She had written that there was work in the cement factory and the steel mills there or iron mining up north. That may not seem too enticing, but you have to remember that at that time I had no other relatives and few friends left to me, and my aunt was always a kind woman. She, too, had no other family there:

20

her new husband died in a mill accident. It's a sad thing to feel alone in the world. No, I never heard another word from or about my uncle in Texas, nor did I ever send any to him.

"But that was some years later. Right after the war I went to a high school in Canton and talked with some teachers there. They got me an appointment with their principal, a Mr. Smithwick. That was in the fall of 1919. After we talked for about an hour, he motioned me to follow, and went room to room and asked some of the teachers to join us at lunchtime. They asked me questions about where I'd been and what I'd done, and the math teacher asked me some questions about algebra and trigonometry. I had used some trig in the war, so that was easy, but some of the algebra, what you couldn't figure out just by reasoning, had me stumped. I could speak French and German better than the teachers, plus my bit of Spanish and Polish and Latin from church—threw in a few Gaelic words just for style. I'd read some history during lulls in the war, books that the people at home had sent over for the soldiers. When we finished lunch, the principal took me back to his office where he got a form from his desk and filled out a Graduation Certificate with my name on it. He said it would help me get a better job. I sent that man a thank-you letter at Christmastime every year until he died.

"I got a job in a metal fabricating plant in Canton and made enough money to pay for college. I did a couple years, but didn't finish. Played football for a year, of all things, and boxed for the college team: they asked me to quit because I couldn't follow the proper rules. Tough thing for a veteran of real fighting, but it helped smooth out my rough technique.

"After about three years in the mill, I got a few days off and went with some buddies to Atlantic City: it was the place to go in those days. One evening I broke up a bar fight—yes, I know I shouldn't have been in there, especially since I didn't drink alcohol, but sometimes you just end up where your buddies go. I'm not perfect—just so you know. Since I settled here, I smoke a cigar every year on my birthday, but only a good one, if I can get it. So: a guy in a fancy European suit stopped me on my way out of the bar and asked me if I wanted to work for the biggest man in town. I didn't say yes or no, but he took me to meet a guy named Nucky Johnson. You ever hear of him? He was suave and offered me good money to protect his interests at one of his hotels. I didn't know at the time that he was the most notorious gangster and bootlegger in Jersey and one of the most powerful on the East Coast. At the time, his boys got me some decent clothes, best I'd ever worn, and he gave me a rent-free apartment in the hotel. After I'd spent a few weeks as little more than a well-dressed bouncer and untrained hotel detective, he called me in one evening and asked if I was ready for something a little bigger. Again I didn't say yes or no, but I knew what he meant. I could see it in his eyes.

"'You want me to waste a guy,' I said.

"He didn't say a word, but the corner of his mouth curled up just a little, and he looked straight at me without blinking.

"I told him how I'd fought in the war and seen enough killing. I told him that if he needed protection, I'd protect him, but if he was having a row with someone over money, I wasn't willing to hurt someone over that. He still said nothing.

"'You've been good to me, Mr. Johnson,' I said, 'and whatever folks say about you, I've never seen anything personally to complain about. I'd like to leave things that way. If you let me walk out that door, I'll leave Atlantic City this instant and cause you no trouble. But I'll ask one favor: don't kill a man over money. It's not worth that. Give him every chance to pay you back, and then give him one more chance.'

"I put my employee ID badge on his desk and looked him straight in the eye.

"He smiled, letting his teeth show. He reached in his coat pocket and pulled out a wad of bills. He took out a hundred-dollar bill—I'd never seen one before—and stretched it across the table to me.

"'Severance pay,' he said. 'I'm sorry to lose you. You're a good man, Hank, and I mean that. Stay that way.' I nodded and turned to leave. 'One more thing: leave that suit you're wearing. You can change back into your old clothes in your apartment. If you leave looking like you do now, someone will think you're one of my boys, and in certain parts of town that wouldn't be safe, even for you. Especially tonight.'

"I nodded good-bye and went right to my apartment, changed my clothes, pulled my hat down over my eyes, and made for the train station. I kept an eye out, but no one followed me.

"It was a dark night, and I kept in the shadows around the back of the station until the train came. Hopped on just as it was leaving and bought my ticket on the train. Took the last seat in the last car by the door, and I got far away with no trouble. A couple days later I saw in a Philadelphia paper that there had been a dust-up in Atlantic City that night, with a couple of men dead. I felt glad I'd missed it.

"Then I heard there was good money to be made in the coal mines in West Virginia. Had a hard time catching on until I got to a place called Scotts Run up around the Pennsylvania border. They hired people from everywhere: hit a vein and needed workers. That held out for almost two years until one day the foreman gave me a dismissal note and said they didn't need me anymore. And that was the end of that.

"I had enough money left to get a train all the way to Arizona. I worked on the Hoover Dam project—now that was something, I tell you. Ever been there? You should go sometime, and see the Grand Canyon, too.

"When they had no more work for me—nobody I knew thought much about long-term work in those days—they let me go, too. Everybody was a 'temp,' and you had to be glad for what you got. Young folks today, even many of the older ones, don't know how bad the Depression was. Not quite bad enough for me to go back to Atlantic City, but bad enough that, even though I took all the decent work I could get, I still had my share of cold and hungry nights.

"I made my way back to Canton, Ohio, hopping trains, but they didn't have any more work for outsiders—hardly enough for locals. I did a little farm and orchard work mostly for the extra food you could get. Not stealing, you understand: they let us do that—what they call *benefits* today. No medical and dental insurance, just a few extra apples and an egg and a piece of bread now and then.

"When I heard there was a factory hiring in Milwaukee, I hitched trains up that way. There was no work by the time I got there. Even dairy farmers wouldn't take me on: they barely had enough for their families. I'm embarrassed to say that I took a couple bare-knuckle fights in the Milwaukee train yards to get a few dollars, and I used that money to get to Waukesha, where I stayed a few days at a boarding house. Sent a letter to my aunt in Duluth, and she replied immediately inviting me there. Hitched the freights through Madison and on, until that evening when I stopped outside Uppsala with no idea what I was getting myself into. That was in the early '30s. That enough background for you?"

"Just right, I think."

"And you're ready for the story you came to hear?"

"I am."

"Sure you're comfortable? Right. Ah: thanks again for that coffee. What I remember most," he said, "is that sound, that unearthly sound—no, that's wrong. Earthly: right up out of the boiling, raging, vengeful, fiery guts of the earth."

ONE

Uppsala, Wisconsin

HOOoooooOOOT! Hoot! Hoot!

The sound of the whistle as the train approached a town. A warning to clear the tracks or to signal the station folk to prepare to load or unload.

I'd heard that sound and other calls like it a thousand times, rolling into and out of railroad yards all over the country.

Some folks may call it a mournful sound, but to me it seemed more hopeful. I was leaving something I needed to leave or heading to something that might be better. That was how I felt on that evening riding that train through Wisconsin. Fall colors had begun to nip at the leaves, but we had had some rain, and everything looked green.

I'd seen the town in the distance, sitting up on a little rise. Not a city, you know, but a town just big enough and just small enough that folks might not resent your stopping there. We'd passed a couple smaller towns, and I figured I'd better jump soon, as I might have been running out of options. It was just into that part of the state where the terrain begins to undulate a little so that it's not so flat. Looked like a nice enough town, a little like parts of northeastern Ohio that I liked, though not quite as green or hilly as that. I'd been slouched in that freight car for long enough. Some of those trains went pretty slowly, with lots of stops. I was lucky never to run into armed guards: some of them took pleasure in beating the hobos, and that wouldn't have gone down well with me. It's hard to get the war out of you once it's got in.

As the train slowed down, I hopped out and hid in the brush until all the cars had passed. When you ride freeload, never get in the first car, the last car, or the middle car—that was always my superstition, and it worked out pretty well.

I had half a chicken sandwich in my coat pocket and a few small coins in my pants pocket. That was all.

The whistle-stop station I was expecting lay just ahead, so I thought I'd picked a good spot.

Then I started walking up toward the town.

The land around the tracks was flat and stony with railroad slag. North of the tracks stood what looked like a telegraph shed—abandoned if it was ever completed—and beyond that a pretty thick wood. I passed underneath the trees and heard before I saw a little waterfall: looked like someone had built it, since the water ran over large, evenly placed stones. The water smelled clean, so I took a chance and had a big drink: I was nearly dead with thirst. The railroad folk didn't serve drinks to hobos. They'd shine your head, not your shoes. I climbed on up over a steep bank and had a look around.

The evening was cool and pleasant with a hint of breeze, the tops of the trees barely moving in time with it. The moon was beginning to rise, and a hint of silver brushed into the eastern sky even as the west was turning to orange and dark blue. When the train had passed out of range, that breeze was the only sound I could hear beyond the faint heartbeat of the waterfall below. Struck me as odd: the town seemed to me to make no sound at all, as if no one lived there. Though the town was above me yet, I stood there for a time and looked around. That place felt peaceful, a feeling I have always valued.

Below, beyond the train tracks to the south, stretched broad, uncultivated fields that disappeared into deep woods. I could just see small plots of cultivated land and a few farm buildings to the southeast. To the east the hill rose briefly, then dipped into a hollow. The breezed turned so that it was coming from the east, and I thought then I could just hear the echo of more substantial running water—turned out that was a river to the northeast. The village climbed the hill to the north. I had no idea yet what was beyond that. If I had, I may have chanced a night's stay in that old telegraph office and hoped for the best, then hopped the next train through to some place far away. To the west the hills rolled in wooded waves off into the sunset. The glens in between might have held almost anything. At the time I would happily enough have leaned my back against a tree, put my jacket over me for a blanket, and slept the night right there. But you couldn't always tell in those days how local folk would feel about that, so I took a couple deep breaths and got going up the hill again.

I'd walked into an unpaved, oak-lined lane that climbed the hill when the thought struck me that I might have picked a deserted town—a fine how-do-you-do, but not unheard of in the Depression. I was hungry and tired and hoped to find a bite and some place to bunk down for the night. But the lane was so pleasant that I stopped again to see the stars emerge. The line of trees on either side curved inward, leaving a straight patch of sky in the middle that was turning cobalt in the growing dusk. I tried to sort out why I felt a reluctance both to stay there and to go on.

Suddenly I realized I had a companion in the road.

It was a small, white dog, some kind of terrier. Probably a mutt, though I don't know dog breeds very well. The dog made a low sound, not quite exactly a growl.

Poor, skinny thing looked like it hadn't eaten in days. I hadn't had much myself, and the dog may have known that. Seemed to me that we had an immediate sympathy for each other.

I knelt down, turned my eyes away, and held my hand out for the dog to sniff if it wanted to.

It came a little closer, but not too close. I gently took the half-sandwich out of my pocket, extracted the bit of chicken from it, and held the meat out toward the dog. Not much of a peace offering, but it was all I had.

The dog got down on its belly and nearly crawled up to my hand. It licked the air a bit, then took the chicken from my hand and backed away. She—I could see then it was a she—rolled over on her side, then back on her belly and ate the chicken in two bites. The round, black eyes stared at me as the tongue kept licking her mouth to get every drop of food, and the tail began to wag rhythmically back and forth. She stayed a few steps away. Smart dog, I thought: don't trust a stranger too much too soon. She didn't ask for any more. I think she knew I didn't have it. I ate the last crust of bread with its slice of tomato and wilted lettuce myself. So we had our day's meal together.

Then I heard the percussion of rapid horse's hooves coming up behind me from down by the tracks and turned to see who it was. I felt like I was about due for some good fortune.

Not likely to be someone from the railroad. Lots of folks rode horses yet outside the cities: either didn't have money for cars, didn't like them, or simply preferred the old ways—and I can't say I blamed them. To this day I'd rather ride a horse than drive a car, even at my age.

Not long till a man came riding, no, blazing up that hill.

His horse was breathing like a bellows, and his hat flew off his head. He didn't even turn around to recover it. I think he would have ridden me down if his horse hadn't reared up in terror. He regained his balance and stared at me.

"You fool, idiot! What are you doing out here? The sun has set!"

I have seen nearly every expression that the face of a human being can make. In the war I was never gassed, nor did I see men in the midst of choking on it. I did see their faces afterwards. I have seen the faces of exceeding joy and excruciating suffering. But I had never seen anything like the way that man's eyes strained and bulged in horror and disbelief.

"What, now, who are you? You don't belong here. Get out! Get out! Do you even know where you are? Are you some kind of thief or madman? Don't expect me to help you! Run, though you can't run fast enough to escape it! Run! Run!"

He lashed his horse till it screeched, and it fired up the road like a flame bouncing up from the rush of embers from steel hammered in the forge.

If the look on his face hadn't shaken me, what I heard next certainly did.

28

In the war I saw some big guns that fired shells that would make the earth shake. I heard bullets whizzing by, humans and animals screaming in pain, dozens of people weeping together with all their souls' last hopes when the war ended. I have heard and seen airplanes crashing from the sky.

I have run toward blazing guns and away from them. In that instant I felt like my feet were riveted to the ground, unable to move from the freezing thrill of utter horror.

I've heard of fight-or-flight, but there are many kinds of fear. The worst kind turns your limbs to jelly so you can't move a muscle.

A wail rose up, a sound such as no human or natural animal could make, something like the siren of a huge fire engine, laced not with warning but with hatred and gall, with ferocity.

WuuuuuuAh! Wah-oooooOOO wah-owwww-eeeeEEEEE! WaaaAAAAH!

It came from far distant, over the hill to the northeast, but it chilled me to the marrow anyway. My muscles went limp, and my teeth began to chatter.

Then, as if in answer, that little dog set up a wail of her own.

Hearing that dog brought me back to life. The dog started to dash away up the road, then stopped to look back at me. Then she dashed away again at full speed.

I heard that awful wail again, farther away than before, but longer and more insistent.

Seeing the dog running brought blood back into my feet and my head. I ran right after that dog as fast as I could go. I passed a small, active farm on my right and then a dead one, its buildings burnt out and the remnant tumbling down. There looked like a stone quarry dropping down the hill to the left, and then maybe a slaughterhouse and an icehouse.

The dirt lane turned left up into a paved road, and the dog followed it. We passed what looked like a couple small businesses, an intersection that spread out in four directions, and a couple more houses, and then a large frame house with a stable and a separate barn on my right.

The dog ran full apace into that barn. The screeching wail came again, closer this time.

Ahead a couple blocks I could see a larger intersection that looked like it broke into streets that spread out in all directions. I had a vague sense of tree-lined lanes beyond that, but had no time to focus on them. That barn looked like the best available choice to me, and I trusted the dog's judgment more than my own, since this was her territory.

Three grim-looking men, two of them with shotguns, had a wagon with a dead buck in the back of it. They left the buck right there in the wagon and two dashed for the front door of the house while the third hurried the horse that had drawn the wagon into the stable. They all moved as if they feared for their lives. Two didn't look back, but the third one slammed closed the stable door and dashed for the house. As he'd entered he'd looked back and seen me. The door closed anyway, and I heard a bolt crack into place. I couldn't tell much in the growing dark, but his expression looked very like that of the man who had passed me on horseback, but more accusatory. No welcome coming from those fellas.

I saw quite a number of buildings ahead.

I saw no other creatures of any sort.

I followed the dog into the barn.

The fading light and the dusty gloom of the barn made seeing much of anything impossible. I was wary of stepping onto tools or into animal droppings. The barn had a couple windows, and as my eyes adjusted to the meager light, I saw the dog, only her eyes and nose, peeking out from underneath a mound of hay.

We both heard that wail again, but this time much louder and closer. It sounded as if whatever it was had followed us up the lane.

The dog looked to me as she glanced, twice, at a rope that fell from the second story of the barn. Then she slid back into the hay, leaving no visible trace of her going. I took the hint and shinnied up that rope, hid myself amidst a few barrels up above.

The barrels all had strong odors, but each was different. One definitely held tar and one lime—that one was partly open. One had a strong salt-water smell, maybe for pickling, but with no smell of food in it—none of them had the faintest whiff of anything edible. A couple held paint, but one of those had a much stronger oily smell. A couple smelled dusty like dry mix for cement. I found a small keg and used it to dip into the lime barrel. Quietly and quickly as I could, I poured some of the lime down the rope that I'd climbed and onto the floor below.

Then came that wail again, loud, long, like the sound of madness incarnate, right outside the door of the barn, which I'd left open.

Wuuuuu UUUUUUUUUU, wawawawaWAAAAAAA, YAAAAAAAAAAA!

I slid behind the barrels and tried not to let my bladder work without my consent. The water I'd drunk at the waterfall below was already weighing on me.

I hoped the dog had hidden herself better than I knew I could do for myself.

A light flickered and seemed to me to scan over the inside of the barn, off the roof and the walls. I could just barely see anything below through a chink between a couple of the barrels. I dared not look down, but plastered myself against the dusty floor, wanting to cover any human scent. We sometimes had to do things like that in the war to keep enemy soldiers from finding us.

Sniffing, and a profound, low growl, like the sound of the deepest base fiddles, with an occasional short, staccato wail that rang in the rafters with hunger and malice . . .

A half moon shone through the window beside me: certainly enough that I couldn't expect to hide in darkness. Perhaps, dark or light, it didn't matter.

I prayed that the lime I'd dropped covered the smell of my tracks.

Something scratching. I hoped the dog wouldn't whimper. She didn't.

Two more quick bursts of that infernal wail. The rafters rang and shook with it.

Then the poles that held up the floor of the second story began to groan.

Whatever was below had begun to climb up. I could hear the chitinous scrape of claws creeping upward.

I could just see the end of the floor through the chink in the barrels. Over the top stretched an enormous, glowing white hand with claws as long as skinning knives. A low growl was slowly amplifying into one of those terrifying, wailing screams, when I heard the dog dash out from under her haystack and out through the front door of the barn.

Whatever had been climbing toward me screeched, and the claw disappeared. The beast let out an angry wail and chased after that poor dog out the door.

I tried to gather my courage to follow the dog and its pursuer, but my limbs felt heavy and weak. It took as great an effort as I ever called up in war to raise myself and look over the top of the barrels.

A faint white light almost like smoke reflecting lantern light whisked itself out the open barn door, and I could still hear heavy breathing just outside. Then the wail rose again, and the sound of feet dashing at more than human or equine speed followed: the creature must have caught sight or scent of the dog and set off to pursue her. I slid down the rope to the barn floor.

Then just as quickly the feet skidded to a halt. The wail gave way to a cry of savage, angry hunger, and I heard the sound of tearing flesh.

It came from the direction of the house that the three men had entered: the beast, whatever it was, had found the dead deer, I guessed—that dog must have led it there on purpose!

Something, maybe my good sense, told me not to look out the door and to stay away from windows. I could hear the steady sound of the tearing of flesh. A growl followed, and another high-pitched, screaming wail, and then I heard the slap of feet running off down the road. I believed in my heart that the dog was off to a much better hiding place than she had before—that way I could also justify not following.

In the rays of moonlight I could spot scratches on the post that whatever that thing was had used to climb up where I'd been hiding: deep incisions from the claws that I myself had seen.

I climbed back up the rope, then dumped a few more casks-full of lime down the rope and onto the floor to cover the smell of my tracks.

You're probably not going to believe this, but when I crawled back among those barrels, the only covering of any sort I could find above the barn floor, the terror had so sucked the life out of me that I fell asleep and lay right there until the sun was well up in the sky.

What woke me wasn't the light, but the barrel of a shotgun poking into my ribs.

I opened my eyes just a crack to see that a man was holding it. He poked again, but as far as I could tell, he didn't have his finger on the trigger.

Quickly as I could I grabbed the end of the gun and yanked it sideways out of his hands.

He was so shocked that he nearly fell backwards off the flooring—it was high up enough that the fall could have killed him. I reached out the butt-end of the gun toward him, and he caught it just before he'd tipped himself over. I gave a tug and pulled him toward me, away from the edge so that he wouldn't fall. Since I didn't know yet who and what sort of man he was, I gave him a shoulder bump in the safe direction, away from the edge—not enough to knock him over, but enough to allow myself to turn the gun around slowly and point the business end away from me and toward him.

He was the man I'd seen entering the house by the barn the night before.

"What are you doing in my barn, pal? We're not looking for any trouble here." He paused as I sized him up. "And what are you intending to do with my gun?"

He looked afraid, and I didn't see any harm in him, so took the shells out of the chambers and returned both gun and shells to their owner.

"I apologize, friend. My name's Hank Peck, though that won't mean anything to you, since I'm not from here. I had no intention at all of spending the night in your barn. But something happened last night that I can't quite explain, and when it was done, I fell asleep before I could choose to do anything more sensible."

He put the shells in his shirt pocket and pointed the gun toward the floor.

"I knew right away you're not from here. Else you wouldn't have spent the night in a barn. You look like a man who knows how to take care of himself, but no one with a stitch of sense would be out here in a barn or in Uppsala at all if he didn't have to be."

"Uppsala, that's the name of this town?"

"You didn't know? Then what are you doing here?" he asked.

"Pure accident. I was enjoying the temporary hospitality of the Milwaukee Railroad, and I needed to stop for food, water, and a bed."

"And you picked here? Then you're either the stupidest or unluckiest man that God ever made. Water's free, but you won't get food or bunk from anyone here, so you'd best get on your way right now. You've got most of the day, and maybe you can catch another train, if you're good at it. Now, don't get riled at me! I'm telling you for your own good."

The fella was about my own age, and he looked sturdy enough, but what I saw in his eyes was fear—not of me, necessarily, but of something.

"You'll be lucky if my brothers don't expect you to pay for that deer carcass out there. We shot it yesterday, and there's nothing left of it. I'll bet you don't have any money anyway."

His look said he hoped I did, but I immediately relieved him of that error. I could see I was going to get no consideration from him—he hadn't even given his name—so I slipped over the edge of the floor and slid down the rope.

"Maybe I can find a little hospitality in town."

"No, you won't. Look, I'm sorry, but that's the way it is here. You forgot your jacket."

He tossed it down to me. I nodded and walked out the door.

Over by the wagon that had held the deer the night before stood two men. One I recognized: he was the man who had nearly ridden me down in the road. Beside him stood a larger man, above six feet tall and broader of build, but with the same facial features. He walked toward me. So I walked toward him, too.

"We don't take to hobos here, fella, and we like thieves even less." He didn't shake my hand, but instead put his on my shoulder and began to grip it tight to show me his strength. I grasped his hand, turned my body aside, and with a trick I learned in the war dropped him right to the ground. I kept stepping back slightly, drawing on his hand so that he couldn't stand up.

I looked over and saw that the third man had pointed his gun at me.

"Put the gun down, Nick," someone behind me said—the man I'd seen in the barn. "He's not going to hurt Lucas while we're both armed."

Slowly Nick let the end of the gun barrel drop toward the ground.

"You vouching for him, Hugh? Do you know who he is? I think he must be crazy."

From behind me I heard Hugh say, "Let poor Lucas up, fella. He won't do any harm if we tell him not to."

I wasn't about to let him do me any harm, but I felt no need to say something foolhardy the way men do in the cowboy pictures. I gave his hand a quick turn so that he spun around on his behind, facing me, and then I yanked him up to his feet. He gave me a look more incredulous than angry.

"What did you say your name is, fella? Hank, is it?" Hugh asked.

"Yes, Hank Peck. Thanks for remembering."

"You're not going to have much reason to thank us, Hank Peck," Nick said.

"Since you gave your name, I'm Hugh McGrath, and that's my brother Nick with the shotgun, and the big one is our brother Lucas."

"I'd like to say 'Good to meet you,' fellas, but so far I can't say I feel especially welcome."

"And you're not welcome," Nick replied.

"But who would be?" Hugh asked him.

"I do apologize, gentlemen, for helping myself to your barn, but I was dog tired, and I must have got some bad water down at the waterfall above the railroad tracks, since I had one whopper of a nightmare."

None of them replied to that.

"That water's fine, Hank, if that's your name, but you'd do best to head right back down to that railroad right now." Nick raised the barrel of his gun just a little, not quite enough to point at my belly. "But before that you'd better pay for that deer."

What the day before had been a deer sat in the road behind the wagon: it was no more than shredded skin and some tangled bones—no flesh, no blood, no remaining recognizable shape.

"I'm not one to stay where I'm not welcome. If you can point me to a place where I can get a little food, and if you can give me a little information, I'll take that advice. I wouldn't pay for that deer even if I had money to do it, as I did neither it nor you any harm."

The gain barrel rose a little so that it faced the middle of my belly.

"No food here for hobos or any other strangers. What information you want?" Nick said.

"Do you know if I can catch a train today, and when?"

"Should be one coming through soon," Hugh said. "Now, leave him alone about the deer, Nick: you know he had nothing more to do with it than Adam. You got any money at all on you, Hank?"

They clearly weren't going to offer me anything, and I understood. I took the few small coins I had in my pocket and showed them to Hugh.

"Not much, poor fella. That may be enough to get you a couple eggs or a sandwich up at the diner. I'll ask Mary to go easy on you. We got a couple other horses here. You going west? Good. I'll ride with you a couple miles up the tracks and drop you off. There's a place where you can probably hop the train pretty easy: the tracks curve through a wood, so they have to slow down, and you can hide where the railroad men won't see you."

"You're telling him too much of our business, Hugh," Nick said. "Just get him outta here and get back as soon as you can."

"Fair enough," I said. "But just one more thing: you'll probably think it stupid, but apparently you already think I'm stupid for being here at all. Last night I thought I saw something—and heard it, too."

"You were dreaming—probably drank some bad whisky and didn't sleep it off on the train." Nick just didn't come across as a caring human being.

"I haven't had whisky since the war, and not much then. And you may be right about a dream. But it didn't feel like that. And there was a little white dog. . . ."

"Cassie!" said the big fellow, Lucas. "You found Cassie?"

"She found me, I think. She led me to your barn. I followed her in mostly because of the sound I heard. Some sort of wailing, like a siren—made my blood run cold."

"If you're a vet like you say you are, then you should be brave enough not to fear strange noises in the dark and run into people's barns." I was liking Nick less and less and felt eager to part his company. "And if you find that stupid dog, you can just take her with you. She's no good for anything and may as well be riding the rails with a hobo."

"I liked that dog," Lucas whined to his brother.

"Since she saw—what she saw—she's been no good for hunting or trapping or anything. Not worth wasting food on, any more than this fella is. Come on: let's get him on his way and see if we can find something to hunt in the woods before the day gets too far along. Look, stranger," Nick said, "you won't believe me, but I'm thinking of what's best for you. Get yourself a hundred miles from here before you even think about poking your head out of a railroad car again. You'll live longer that way, and I'm not talking about no gun."

Nick put the barrel of the gun over his shoulder and turned and went into the stable.

"Come on, Hank," Hugh said. "Let's see if we can get you a bite at the diner and get you on your way. You'd do best to forget anything you think you saw or heard here. Mary's a good cook, and she'll wrap up something you can take on your way."

Hugh put his gun against the barn door and motioned toward the center of town, and I followed.

Lucas said something in a loud whisper, and I could hear it plain as birdsong.

"Do you think she saw it, Nick? Do you think she saw Wiskalo Chookalo? She'll be a mad dog if she did! Do you think *he* saw, the stranger?"

Nick cursed and spat. "Shut up, you miserable fool! How could our father produce such a stupid son! Go on, get your traps and let's go or I'll leave you alone in the woods and you can find your own way out!" Nick hadn't singled me out for abuse. He gave it to his brother as well.

"Don't do that, Nick. I'm ready. I'm ready—just got to get my traps."

Hugh had got well ahead of me, and he didn't turn around. I walked quickly to catch up. I wondered if I had heard right, the words were so odd. I had a sense that if I asked Hugh what that name—*Whisky* something—meant, he'd tell me he had no idea, and that I must have misheard his unfortunate brother.

I also really wanted to get another look at that dog.

Then I heard footsteps behind me and turned to see.

About thirty paces back stood Cassie the dog, her tail wagging eagerly.

TWO

Unfortunate Timing

The center of town looked clean enough, if a bit lost in time. The lanes spread out in a rectangular grid with houses of various sorts, some older but some newer: frame bungalows, craftsman ranches, two-story squarish structures with stone façades—none taller than that. Down the main street I spotted a market with dry goods, a good-sized modern bank, and a post office that looked closed. Except for the bank, it could have been 1933 or 1905.

I followed Hugh into a small diner. It didn't even have a marquee out front. Probably everyone in town already knew about it, and apparently they didn't encourage outsiders to find it. The smell of cooked food almost caused me to pass out—I had eaten only a little more than half a sandwich in the last two and a half days.

The diner had only half a dozen tables and a counter in front that would seat eight. Two men sat at the counter, and a couple, both maybe sixty years old, sat at one of the tables. No one was talking. No one turned around when we came in.

The woman behind the counter poured coffee for the two men sitting there. She looked up and saw us standing a few feet from the counter. "Oh," she said, and she dropped her coffee carafe on the counter. It was heavy and empty, and it didn't break.

The others turned to look. The woman at the table uttered a muffled shriek.

"Good morning, Hugh," she said, but she was looking straight at me with astonishment in her face.

"A stranger," Hugh said. "He'll be on his way out of town as soon as he gets something to eat. He has some money, and I'll pay the rest."

One of the men at the counter was about to get up.

"Don't bother," I said, and tapped him on the shoulder. "I'll get right out of your way."

He growled, but didn't speak.

"Mary, is it? My name's Hank Peck. I mean no trouble. I stopped here by mistake, and I just need a little food and I'll be on my way."

"A little food," she said, and her face contorted as she tried to smile. That face looked like it hadn't smiled in a very long time. That wasn't unusual in those days, still deep in the Depression, but something else swept across her features: deep distrust, deep worry, or both.

"Get the man a glass of water, Mary," Hugh said. "And make something that you can do quickly. We've got to get him to where he can get on the train and move along."

"Hobo," said the man who had almost got up from the counter.

"Take it easy, Galen," Hugh said.

"I've heard worse names," I said. "But these days a person's not always at fault for being poor. Maybe folks would find it easier to help one another if they could see a stranger as a friend in need rather than an enemy looking to do harm."

"We don't need no friends here," Galen said. "We need ignorant folk from elsewhere to stay away and mind their own business."

I made ready in case Galen was intending to do more than just talk, but Mary, recovering herself, saved us both some trouble.

"Now don't you worry, Galen, or Hugh: I'll just make an egg sandwich in no time. Here's some cold water, and I'll poor you some coffee—got it in the back. I can chop a few carrots in no time, too, for Mr. . . ."

"Peck, ma'am, and thank you very much. I don't have much money, though. I'd be willing to do some work to pay off my bill if you could spare a bit more."

"No time for work, Hank. Pay what you have, and I'll pay the rest, and let's get you going," Hugh said.

"Going: best idea I've heard yet," Galen muttered.

Mary nodded and disappeared through a swinging door. I drained my water glass and motioned to Hugh that I was going to sit at one of the tables closest to the window, away from the counter.

There just outside the door stood Cassie the dog, her eyes wide and her tail wagging hopefully.

"Any chance we can turn up a little piece of meat for the dog, Hugh?" I asked.

"Don't be worrying about that mangy little dog. We had to throw her out after she got a look at—well, she went kind of crazy, so we don't feed her anymore. Don't want to encourage a crazy dog to stick around."

"But she used to hunt with you," I said.

"*Used to* is right. Not anymore."

"But if she's your dog, shouldn't you do something to take care of her?"

Mary placed full cups of coffee in front of both of us. I took a sip gladly.

"None of your business, Hank. I'm getting tired of having both of you around, so as soon as Mary gets that food, you're getting out of here. And feel welcome to take the dog with you."

"All right, Hugh. No harm intended. I have only one more question for you."

He looked at me, but didn't ask me what it was. I could tell he didn't want any questions, but my curiosity was up, and I had to ask.

"Who or what is 'Whisky Chuck'?"

I heard Mary gasp from behind the counter. Hugh's face turned white, and an angry look rose in his eyes. Galen at the bar laughed with a single loud guffaw.

"I say we get this boy outta here now," Galen said, pushing back his chair. "This is no place for idiots." He got up and came over to stand beside me—too close for my preference.

"No sandwich, no vegetables. No need even for you to walk: I'll carry you out myself. Get up, boy."

I never like to hear a man call another man *boy*. A lot of the white

41

men I knew when I was growing up and in the army had done that to black men as a matter of course, and it always made me sick. Treat a man like a man, and you'll make a friend. Treat a man like a boy, and you'll make an enemy for life. I sat still and didn't even turn my face to him.

"Better leave him alone, Galen," Hugh said.

Galen thrust a fist toward my face, stopping just short. "Didn't you hear me, boy?" he added for emphasis. Then he pushed his fist into my jaw, causing me to knock over my coffee cup.

I can be patient when I need to, but any man has limits, especially anyone not accustomed to getting bullied. Without standing—he was too close to me—I recovered my balance, turned his fist aside, and stuck a short, straight punch into his solar plexus.

He sighed loudly and unconsciously took a step back from me. I got up and grabbed the front of his shirt with both hands and drew downward, swinging a knee up into the point of his chin—not too hard—as his head came down. Then I eased him, unconscious, onto the floor so that neither of us broke anything.

I heard the cock of a gun and turned to face Galen's friend at the counter, who had pulled a Smith & Wesson on me.

Hugh politely stepped in front of me with both his hands raised.

"Galen had that coming, Joe, so let's just leave it at that. Hank, you do seem to get yourself into deeper and deeper trouble. You got that food ready, Mary? Hank and I are going to take a ride down to the railroad. Come on, Joe: put that gun away. That's a good fella. We're all a little too touchy today."

"Sorry about your friend," I said. "He'll be all right. Just a bit of a headache when he wakes up."

Joe reluctantly returned his gun to its holster. Mary hurried out and put a small bag into my hands. She grasped both of my hands as she did it and looked into my eyes.

"Good luck, stranger—Hank—and I hope you find better hospitality somewhere else than you found here."

"Thanks very much, Mary, and no harm done. Ready, Hugh. Lead on."

42

When we went out, I closed the door behind me, and there was Cassie, looking up expectantly and wagging her tail. The lunch bag Mary had given me felt fuller than I'd expected. I looked in, and addition to an egg sandwich and some sliced carrots, I found some thin slices of beef, a small apple, and two large oatmeal cookies. I took one of the beef slices and held it down to the dog. She gobbled it down as happy as if all were right with the world.

"Let's get those horses," Hugh said, "and if we don't get you out of town soon, I really do suspect someone's going to shoot you, and no one but kind-hearted Mary will feel the least bit sad about it."

"Not even you?" I asked. "You stepped between me and a gun back there."

"Just trying to be polite," Hugh answered. "You haven't seen much politeness here, and I'm sorry for it. But that's the way things are."

"Yes," I said, "it's been a long while since I felt welcome anywhere."

The center of town, just past the diner, had a cobblestone street that ran up the hill to the north and down the hill to the south. The central part of the town sat pretty flat.

"What's to the north of town, over the hill?" I asked Hugh, as we began to walk back toward his barn.

"You don't need to know, since in a few minutes you're leaving and never coming back."

"I'm just curious. Most of what I've seen of Wisconsin isn't land like this. The terrain here reminds me of parts of northern Ohio that I used to know."

"Ohio? That where you're from? Why show up here?"

"As I told you: just passing through—on my way to Duluth to find work."

"Ever been through West Virginia, up in the mountains?"

"Not so much in the mountains. I dug coal up north near the Pennsylvania border."

"That Scotts Run?"

"Yes, that's it. You've been there?"

"No, we, my brothers and me, came from the mountains down south, not far from Virginia. We came here—to buy some nice farm land

43

cheap. Look, don't ask me too many questions, because I don't want to get to know you. Beyond the hill there's woods, a stream, and a dell, and beyond that another rise with a forest and a marsh, then a good-sized lake. That's more than you need to know."

At the barn Hugh asked if I knew how to saddle a horse. I did. He led his horse, already saddled, and I prepared mine and followed. He took a Winchester rifle and slung it over his back.

We rode down to the railroad tracks—a shortcut through the woods, not the way I had come up the evening before—and we turned west and north as soon as the ground flattened out. We didn't speak a word for some time.

"So, Hugh, about this *Whisky Chuck* . . ."

"That's not it. Where'd you hear that, anyway?"

"Your brother Lucas said it."

"Lucas said it?"

"*Whispered* more than *said*. When you were leading me toward the diner."

"You can forget about Whisky Chuck. No such person."

"You said I didn't say it right. That means it's somebody. Look: what I thought I saw last night—was that Whisky Chuck? And what is it? Not a man, certainly."

"You fought in the Great War, Hank?"

"Yes. In France and in Belgium."

"Saw your share of action?"

"And then some."

"Learned to kill men and what it means to be killed? Killed by something horrible, bombs, fire, gas?"

I didn't reply. Some questions don't require answers.

"Yes, you did. You also learned that there are some things in the world that we're better off not knowing about."

He whipped his horse and galloped ahead of me. I kept my own pace. He could hurry if he wanted to. I caught up to him after a bit.

"How many people live in Uppsala?"

"About five hundred. Used to be more like a thousand, long time ago. Won't be one more today or any time soon. Look: the last time we had

44

a stranger in town, little more than a year ago, two Uppsalans died, and nobody—I mean *nobody*—went out-of-doors after dark for months."

We rode around a big bend in the railroad tracks into an s-curve that ran between two steep, wooded banks.

"Here's the spot we're looking for. Perfect place to board the train. They have to slow down here, and you can hide and then jump on without much trouble. You'll be long gone before nightfall."

I got off the horse and handed Hugh the reins.

"Look what followed us," Hugh said in some disgust.

It was Cassie the dog. She stopped about thirty yards behind us and sat down.

"Poor, stupid critter," Hugh said. "You ever taken a dog on a train?"

"Once, at the request of a friend. They're good company, but they get hungry and thirsty, and they need relief the same as we do. They make itchy hobos."

"You may as well take her with you if she'll go. If she don't, I'm going to shoot her."

"Why would you do that?"

"You haven't got the idea yet that it's not safe around here. I suppose you think we're all just a bunch of bad-tempered hayseeds. Listen good, and get this: I'm getting you on that train for your own good. If you stay here, you're as good as dead. If that dog stays, she's dead, too, and maybe I am, and I'm not quite ready for that yet."

"Whisky Chuck?"

"I'm not telling you anything more. I'm going to ride up onto that low ridge to the north, where I can see you, and I'm going to watch you get on that train. If you and that dog aren't on it, I'm going to shoot either or both of you. Meantime, I suggest you hide in the trees right there, where I'm pointing. Good-bye and happy life to you, Hank Peck, if such a thing still exists in this world."

Hugh found a small, clear path and rode right up the hill into the trees. After a bit I saw him emerge on the ridge up above. He pointed with his finger to the spot he had shown me before, beneath some brush. Then he took his rifle and held it in both hands in front of him, still as a statue. I slipped under the low brush and sat with my legs

45

crossed. In an instant that little white dog jumped into my lap, panting hard, her tail wagging.

Not more than a couple minutes later I heard the hoot of the train—it must just then have been coming into the whistle-stop station below Uppsala. It must not have stopped, because very shortly it turned into the curve where Hugh, Cassie, and I were waiting, each with our own thoughts and purposes.

As the train neared, I crouched, ready to jump on at the best opportunity. But I could see plainly standing on the front footboard behind the railing was a uniformed armed guard. Across his chest he held a Thompson semi-automatic. He looked straight ahead—didn't seem to see me. But I wasn't taking chances. I waited.

Not a long train, only about a dozen cars, but it must have been carrying something important—or they were cracking down on hobos. When the two middle cars went by, I could see through the open doors a couple men crouching with Browning rifles. Still no chance to board. As they passed, one of the men looked out: he must have spotted me in the brush. I heard a long, sharp whistle.

As the caboose passed, another uniformed guard stood looking right where I crouched. He pointed his Thompson at me. Then, as the car passed, he made a gesture with his hand that I won't describe.

I had no chance to get on that train, and before long it had disappeared into the west.

The dog looked at me, and I looked at her. Neither of us knew what to do.

I stepped out onto the tracks and looked up at the ridge above: Hugh was still there sitting on his horse, but his gun was pointing down toward me.

A bullet whizzed by about ten feet to my right. He motioned with his gun that I should follow the train to the west. When I didn't move, another bullet by whizzed by, this one about five feet to my right. That seemed to satisfy him that he had got his message across, and he turned and rode on and up to the east, back toward Uppsala.

Things got pretty quiet then. All I could hear was Cassie's light panting and the *ping, ping* sound of a cardinal in a tree not far away.

I sat down beside the track and took from my jacket pocket the lunch bag that Mary had made for me. Cassie made some eager sounds, scanning my face and my bag hopefully but politely. I gave her a couple more strips of beef and ate the egg sandwich myself.

Then I ate the carrots and one of the oatmeal cookies. I put the rest back in my pocket.

I had no idea what lay to the west: I might have to walk for hours into nothing but darkness. Didn't make any sense to go back to Uppsala. Probably too far to try to find one of those towns east of Uppsala, and I didn't know if Hugh might be waiting down that way with his Winchester loaded and ready. That decided me. Start south, to get out of view, then turn back east and try to make one of those farms south of town—at least I knew something was there. I certainly couldn't wait where I stood for dark to come, maybe bringing Whisky Chuck, or whatever it was, back for a second chance at me.

I followed the track to where the s-curve began, then turned south through light trees and brush into a long, rough, uncultivated field. Cassie followed me. After a while we turned east, kept a good pace, wanting to find something before dark.

We walked through the whole afternoon, until I saw the large farm I had passed the day before. I had a feeling to make for the smaller farm just south and east of that. Dusk was just dropping over us when we reached it. The best strategy seemed to me to walk right up to the front door.

I heard the sound of someone cocking a gun.

I dropped my coat, which I'd been carrying. Cassie made a growl, but I held my palm toward her, making a "down" signal, hoping that would work with a dog I barely knew. It did. Then I held my hands above my head.

"No harm, friend," I said. "I'm going to turn around slowly. I have no weapon, and I'm not here for any reason other than accident. I'm happy just to keep going if you don't take kindly to strangers."

A man emerged from behind a utility building. He had a nice-looking Colt handgun directed at my middle. He was a little taller than I and a little darker of skin. He had a round face with black hair, wore it rather long, tied in the back, and he had attentive eyes. He held a pair of work gloves in his other hand. When he stepped toward me, his footfalls made no sound. He stopped and looked at me for what must have been a minute or two but seemed much longer, since I was standing there with hands over my head and looking him and his Colt right in the eye. Finally he spoke.

"You're a soldier, or were. Army. You don't scare easy. You've done some boxing, bare-knuckle, I'd guess. You haven't eaten much lately, but you had something today. You're not from here—somewhere east, but not East Coast. You need a place to stay. You fought in Europe? Who with?"

"US 3rd Infantry. Flanders and France: Ypres, Marne, others. You too?"

"Ha. How'd you know?"

"Same way you did: last round of Army-issue boots. You've got the heavy ones, better for farm work. I have the lightest I could get: better for travel."

"I signed up in Canada in '15."

"I went the same way in '17."

"Hobo?"

"Wasn't till I fell out of work."

"Things still bad out east? You got that jacket in Philadelphia."

"Right again." I could follow most of his deductions, but that one escaped me.

"Me, too," he said, "3rd Infantry. "I don't remember you, though."

"Big outfit."

"You see Rickenbacker on 11/11?"

"Yes."

"That was something. He loved his old Curtiss."

"He flew a SPAD III. I put my fingers in the bullet holes a few days later."

I'd passed my test.

"You know the man?"

"Never met him. How about you?"

"Naw, he wasn't interested in Indians like me."

"Oneida?"

He made a low sound that reminded me of a laugh. "How'd you know?"

"Lucky guess from my college history course."

"College man, eh?"

"Two years. Then back to work. While it lasted."

"I did three and a half years at Madison, studying agriculture, until a dean found out I'm Indian, and he made sure they got rid of me. Where'd you work?"

"All over: Ohio, Texas, New Jersey, New York, West Virginia, Illinois and Colorado just passing through, Arizona. More yet on my way back. I'm heading for Duluth, Minnesota. My aunt's there, and she wrote me that they have work for men who want it."

"Then you were walking the wrong way, if you want to go to Duluth."

My turn to laugh.

I felt a cold wind as the sun set, and I shivered unconsciously.

"Truth is that I just got off the train in the wrong spot."

"Right. Pick up your coat and bring your dog," he said. "Let's go inside the house. Nights are getting a little cold early this year, and it's not safe to be outside after dark around here."

"I know."

"You know?" he asked. "Come in. My sister made some coffee and biscuits, and you can tell me about what you think you know."

"Hank Peck."

"Daniel Cornelius," he replied and offered me his hand. "Call me Dan. Come on, Hank. Daylight's all but gone. Dog can come, too."

He walked to the back door of the house, and Cassie and I followed.

THREE

Stories, True and Otherwise

My thoughts drifted back to the night before. I shivered again—not something I do very often—and only partly from the cold.

The house looked like it had been built in stages. Most of it was wood. Part had a second floor, and two additions made of stone poked out at unusual spots. It gave a sense of being both old and sturdy and at the same time a work in progress.

The smell of coffee poured out as soon as Dan opened the door. The rich, earthy warmth put life back into my limbs even before we entered. The smell of fresh biscuits mixed with it and settled it down at about face height from the floor, and I noticed I was still hungry even though I'd eaten that day.

The kitchen had a high ceiling. Tall cupboards reached most of the way up. Large windows pointed east and south. As soon as Dan stepped in, he drew blinds down over them.

A round table with six chairs sat right in the middle of the room. The walls were decorated with all sorts of things: woven blankets, ritual masks, a couple paintings, one of a winter lake scene and one of a stag looking out from a ridge. Kitchen utensils hung in convenient places, and a couple washtubs had been pushed into one corner. A woman stood facing away from us working at a counter.

"Brought a friend," Daniel said.

"Two," she corrected. "No friends likely to show up at this time of day," the woman replied, not turning around, "but they're welcome anyway." Cassie settled down to sentry beside the door.

"Thanks for making the fresh biscuits. We're going to need the extra. Thought we might," Dan said.

"What made you think that?" the woman asked.

"Don't know, he said. "Just thought it. Thoughts like that usually turn out right."

He motioned for me to sit by the table, and then he opened a pantry door and pulled out a large bowl of vegetables and looked around. "Ah, good," he said, "we've still got some strips of venison. Thank you, brother deer." He put them on the table, then gathered glasses and a large pitcher of water.

The woman repeated the thank-you, then turned around with a large platter covered with biscuits, butter, jam, and dried fruits. She put a blanket on the floor for Cassie, along with two little dishes, one with some milk and one with a little meat.

She had a calm, round face like her brother's, but her skin was darker. She had a thin nose and round eyes that looked very old for someone so young. She was very nearly his height, and she moved with the same silent steps, but she must have been a few years younger. I guessed Daniel to be about my age or a bit older, given his war experience, but she looked more like early twenties.

I'd sat where Dan had motioned me, but I stood reflexively as she got to the table. She had something regal about the way she moved. "Thanks for accepting me into your house. Everyone's wary of strangers anymore, but around here folks seem especially so. You don't need to worry about me. I don't have any more money, but I can work to pay off food and bunk, if you'll allow me."

"You always talk a lot?" she asked.

"This is Hank Peck, Sis. He's been about everywhere, including France and Belgium, 3rd Infantry with me. Hank, this is my sister, Polly Cooper."

"How do you do," I said, and she nodded.

I thought her name sounded familiar, again something from one of my history classes, Revolutionary War, maybe. To be that Polly Cooper she'd have to be about a hundred seventy years old, but she might well be a descendant.

"Wasn't there a Polly Cooper in the American Revolution?" I asked.

"I'm named for her," she said. She pointed me back down in my chair, and we all sat down together. They closed their eyes, so I did, too.

"Let us put our minds together and thank Mother Earth, who cares for all lives. Earth gives us food, water, medicine, and strength to live. For what the Creator gives us, we are always thankful."

Her prayer took me back to memories of my own. I had got out of the habit after the War. War leads some people to prayer, but it takes prayer away from others.

Dan turned off all the lamps except for one that he placed in the middle of the table. He lit three candles on the countertops.

They passed around plates, glasses, and food, and the three of us ate hungrily and in silence for some time. I couldn't remember the last time I had a proper meal sitting at a table with other people.

"You have family besides the aunt in Duluth?" Dan spoke at about the time that I thought no one was going to say anything more. I didn't know Oneida customs, so I intended not to say much until someone suggested I do otherwise.

"Not many anymore. I think my uncle is still alive, working in the Texas oil fields, if they're even operating now. Parents died years ago. No siblings. Some cousins in Ohio, but I never got to know them very well."

"It's good to have family," Polly said. "The Creator must take care of those who don't."

I sat and thought for a while. "I had a wife. Married a girl in France after the war, but she died in the influenza epidemic in '18."

I noticed Dan was looking me right in the eye. His eyes glimmered with the reflection from the oil lamp.

"So did I," he said. "She came back with me, but—things were tough on her here."

"She loved you, and she loved the farm," Polly said. "People here aren't easy."

"She's gone, too?" I asked.

"Yes," he said. "We don't . . ."

"Yes," I said.

After a time Dan said, "We don't use spirits—alcohol, that is— Hank, so I can't offer you some."

"That's all right," I said. "I don't use them either, not since the war anyway. When I was in Milwaukee I'd have a beer now and then—the men I worked with drank it like water. I like to keep a clear head, and even beer can muddy my thinking. Clarity kept me awake in the war, and it helped me stay alive. I have the idea that it still can."

"Good," Dan said, and Polly nodded her assent.

"The coffee's good," Dan said. "You notice the chicory in it, Hank?"

"Ah, so that's the flavor I noticed."

"Don't be too hard on the people here, Hank," Polly said. "They have reasons for why they are what they are."

"I understand. Not all good people are friendly people. I got the sense that folks over in Uppsala especially don't like strangers."

"You were in Uppsala?" Dan asked. "When?"

"Last night. And this morning." I hazarded a question. "If you don't mind, there's something I'd like to ask you about that place."

"Not tonight," Dan said.

We talked quietly for a bit, then sat listening to the wind blow against the side of the house. Without saying anything we all got up together and cleared the table and cleaned the dishes. I'm not sure why, but I almost felt like one of the family—maybe because their welcome was simple and unforced, almost nonchalant.

"I'm going to put out the oil light now, Hank," Dan said. "Take one of the candles. You can probably get an hour or so out of it yet. There's a couch in the study where you can sleep. It's right in the middle of the house, with no windows. You'll find a couple piles of books there, if you're interested, and a couple extra candles to read by—just remember to put them out before you fall asleep. There's a bunch of agriculture books that probably won't interest you—they're left over from college and probably out of date by now. There's a Christian Bible, an old one with some of my study notes in it. There's a copy of *Pilgrim's*

Progress—a guy gave that to me at the University. I think he wanted to convert me to Methodism. Some Dickens novels, *A Tale of Two Cities* and *Hard Times*—yeh, I actually thought about being an English major. A couple craft books on woodworking, and a few dime novels that I picked up during the war, even a couple books in French that I got there—*L'homme qui Rit*, a really strange book by Hugo. You should be able to find something. Or with all the walking you did today, you may just want to sleep. I'm going fishing in the morning. Come along if you get up early enough."

"You both talk too much," Polly said. "Let Hank sleep. It's time, well past time, for quiet here."

I checked Cassie: she had fallen asleep on the kitchen floor.

Dan led me down a low hallway to the study. The couch already had a blanket on it, which I unfolded. I found the Hugo novel and picked it up. He lit a second candle.

"Two basins under the couch: one empty and one with fresh water. Comfortable?" Dan asked.

"Plenty," I said. "Thank you."

"No need to thank me. Hospitality's everyone's right. Thank the Creator for that."

"I will. I do."

Dan saluted and closed the door behind him when he went out.

That night I felt very fortunate. I sat down to read.

My French was rusty. I got through only a page or two—hard to read by candlelight. I just remembered to put out the candles before a huge wave of exhaustion swept over me. I dropped onto the couch— fell asleep on my way down.

I woke once, dreaming of something shapeless, malicious, glowing blue-white. I imagined that a claw slipped under the door and crept toward me. I was too tired to move, too tired to wake, too tired to struggle, and fell back into an even deeper sleep.

When I woke again, the room was still dark. I felt better, like I had slept for a long time, but I had no notion of the time: the room had no windows and so no light. Not even a blink of light under the study door.

I got up slowly, moved carefully toward the door, and found the knob without knocking over anything.

There was a dim, gray light in the hallway, and I turned in the direction that I remembered as moving toward the kitchen. As I went that way, the hallway got brighter. The kitchen had a yellow glow: the sun was well up, the blinds opened, and lighted poured in both windows. But no one was there. They'd left one of the windows wide open: apparently they didn't worry about anyone getting in during the daylight.

A note lay on the table along with a large carafe, a bowl of fresh and dried fruit, and a half-loaf of dark bread with a large pat of butter. The note read: "Have a bite. There's some wood to chop out back, and you can dump the used basins outside beyond the fence and refill the clean ones at the spring that's just over the hill to the south. We'll talk when I get back. –DC." The carafe of coffee was room temperature, but I didn't mind. I poured a cup of that first and drank it down with pleasure, then chased a mouthful of bread and dried apples and fresh berries with another long drink. I found basins in front of several doors in the house and, along with those from the study, either emptied and washed or refilled them. Then I went out back to take care of the other chores.

They'd already let Cassie out. I didn't look for her: she must have gone into the trees to fend for herself. An axe was stuck upright in the ground next to some hefty logs that were spread about. I had those chopped and stacked by the back door in about an hour. I noticed where out front one of the fence posts had tumbled over, so I got some tools from the utility shed and made it and the fence upright and sturdy again. Found an otherwise pretty good shovel with a bent blade, so I hammered it back to true and cleaned it. I was about to look for something else to do when Polly came walking up toward the front of the house from the field below.

"Good day to you, Miss Cooper."

"No 'miss,' just 'Polly Cooper.' Everyone calls me Polly Cooper."

"Both names?"

"Right. You had any lunch?"

"No. I had breakfast."

"Come on." I was thinking how unusual it would feel to have more than one meal in a day.

I followed her to the back door. "You do nice work," she said.

"Thank you."

"Dan will be back soon. He may have a fish or two. Catfish taste pretty good if you cook them right."

No sooner did she say it than Dan hopped over the fence with a string of a few nice-sized catfish in one hand and fishing gear in the other.

"Thank the river for today's meal," he said. "Some people say the catfish is an ugly creature, but they're good if you cook 'em right."

Polly smiled at him and nodded and led us both into the house. The sky was beginning to cloud over.

Dan pulled a frying pan out of a cupboard and threw some butter and herbs and a touch of salted water in it. He nodded to me to watch the pan while he went out back to scale the fish.

I wasn't accustomed to eating so often. A fella can get used to that sort of thing, but getting used to anything in those days amounted to a bad habit.

Dan fried the fish, while I cleaned the mushrooms, an onion, and some root vegetables that Polly had dug up. She cooked those, and I went out to the spring for some more water. When I got back, Cassie was waiting by the door, and the meal was ready. Polly put a little meat and a few vegetables in a small bowl for the dog and left it outside by the step. Cassie gave me a joyful look that said "I don't get food like this either!"

Dan and Polly prayed as they had the night before. I bowed my head and listened. Then they began a low chant in a language I didn't recognize—found out later it was Oneida, which they told me the people were losing: few people spoke it regularly anymore, though those who knew it passed it on to their children. Sad: it had a slow, pensive beauty, a roughly rhythmical music unlike any language I'd heard.

We ate for a while in silence. They weren't great talkers, and in those days neither was I.

Cassie scratched at the door, and Polly let her out.

Finally Dan looked me in the eye. "Ask your question," he said.

I knew what he meant, and I guessed that he anticipated my question.

"I'd like to know about something one of the men in Uppsala said. I didn't hear him clearly: he more spat the words than spoke them. It sounded like a name: *Whisky Chuck*, or something vaguely like that."

"Whisky Chuck! That what he said? Never heard of that."

"Is that what you heard, or are you trying to make something sensible out of words you didn't know?" Polly asked.

"Well, you're right. That's not exactly it. If I just think back to the sounds—it was more like 'Wisklo Chookle.' That's as close as my memory can get to it. Does it mean anything to you?"

They sipped on their chicory coffee for a time and said nothing. I almost thought they were going to ignore my question. Finally Dan sighed.

"*Wiskalo Chookalo*: is that what the man said?"

"Yes, that might well have been it. What does it mean?"

"White people's words," he said, looking at Polly. "No offense, Hank. Look: you're a brave man. One knows another. You've been around, and you've seen a lot. But I doubt you've seen anything like this. Are you sure you want to know?"

"I've already seen something. I'd like to know what it was."

"Tell me as exactly as you can what you saw," Dan said, his eyes trained on mine.

So I told them my adventure of two nights before in as much detail as I could remember, trying to stay brief and not to embellish. I hadn't done anything heroic. I just told the truth as I could recall it. They both sat riveted as I spoke.

"He saw it all right," Polly said.

"What did I see?"

"You're a lucky man, Hank Peck, to have survived it. So you didn't get a look straight at it? You didn't see its eyes?"

"I saw blue-white light among shadows and a clawed hand that a lion would envy. I don't think it saw me, but it must have smelled me. It got a look at Cassie, though. She's one brave lass. She probably saved my life by leading it away from me."

"It doesn't usually go for animals, or so they say," Dan said. "Sometimes for dogs, though, especially brave ones that dare to stand up to it. Not many creatures will. That's if the creature is even real. I still don't even know for sure, though I trust that you saw something very strange, Hank. I haven't seen it myself. It doesn't bother Indians. When it comes, it stalks white men."

"The name: what does it mean?"

He made a sound like a laugh.

"English corruption of Oneida words. Our people called it *owiskla niwashohkot tshukalol*, or maybe someone said *wiskliyo tshuhkalo*— that's where the white people got their name for it. Our words are sometimes hard for them. I've heard it called *ohsuhta'ko atyanlusla* by some of the old people: that means "spirit of the great darkness" in English. Some of the Mamaceqtaw—the people the whites call Menominee—know about it. They call it *waapeskiw meswaew*. I don't know that they've seen it that far north, where most live now, but stories get around. The ghost seems to want to stay right around here." He was almost smiling.

"You call it a 'ghost.'"

"Best I can do in English."

"You don't want to tell me what it means."

"You won't like it."

"Dan, it's itching me, and whether I'll like it or not, I want to know."

"*White rabbit.*"

"What about a white rabbit?"

"That's what the words mean: *white rabbit.*"

"Seriously?"

"Seriously."

"Then that's not what I saw. That was no white rabbit."

"You said you didn't see it clearly."

"It was big. It was angry. It wailed like a thousand banshees. It ran like a whirlwind. It had a hand as big as the hub cover on an automobile tire. That was no rabbit."

"Of course it wasn't. That's just what the *On'yote'aka*, the Oneida, call it. Partly to make fun of the white people. But they say it runs faster than the fastest horse, has long legs and feet and long ears that hang down. It's no rabbit: that's just a name."

"Where did it come from, the ghost?"

"The legends say it came right up out of the earth, some kind of chthonic spirit."

"Why? What brought it, or who?"

"Before the English, Scots, Germans, and Irish settled here," Dan explained, "Uppsala was settled by Swedes and Dutch, other Northerners from Europe. The name of the place comes from a town in Sweden—that's not what we called it. Some of the land the Swedes bought from the Oneida, and some they shared with us—they were few, and we let them settle, and they let us work and trade there. Before long their families followed them, and then their friends, and we got more than we'd bargained for. The new folk coming in didn't appreciate the Oneida ways, and some of us who had families over here south and east or even elsewhere in the state just moved out. Others stayed and remained part of the town.

"The real problem came with the next settlers—that's too nice a name to call them. They were British and German, came from out East and from the mountains in the South, West Virginia and Tennessee and Kentucky, thereabouts, in a wagon train. First they drove out the Oneida with fire and rifles. The Norse folk: the newcomers just wouldn't do business with them and even stole from them. Later they simply overwhelmed them: greater numbers and a lot meaner. They'd set fire to people's homes at night, find them in the woods and beat them or worse. Bought out their land and homes for next to nothing. Nasty lot. The Norsemen eventually just moved along, those that survived.

"That was when it—Wiskalo Chookalo—first appeared. My grandfather talked with a Dutchman who called it *verdrukker:* means something like 'dragger' or 'drawer,' a materialized ghost that will draw people down into the earth with it. The Icelanders had stories about those, too. A Finn called it *valkoinen aavt:* 'white ghost.' The ones who stayed called it the name you heard, which they got from us because of the way they described it. They say one dare not look at it, and you had better not let it look at you—a little like Medusa or the cockatrice in Greek myth. It pursues and kills—and eats, they say—anyone who confronts it or happens to get in its way or look it in the eye."

"If it's so deadly, who lives to describe it?"

"A few have seen it, or so they say. Glimpses, or a few lucky folk who escaped it at sunrise got away, at least for a time. It never comes out in the light. And it doesn't come out every night. When it does come out, by dawn it disappears back into the ground. But once it sees you, it may come back every night until it catches you."

"I wouldn't have believed in it if I hadn't seen it. Cassie the dog escaped it! Apparently the deer carcass distracted it."

"Yes, most people wouldn't believe it exists, and few in Uppsala would believe the dog got away. I don't know. I'm still not sure it isn't some disguise for white men's mischief rather than a real ghost."

"Why hasn't someone tried to kill it?"

"People have. None of those lived to tell about it. Their neighbors caught those glimpses. And they heard it, that long, foul, hideous wail. You heard it. Did you stick around to face it?"

"Yes, I heard it, all right. What draws it out?"

"Violence, hunters with guns—other than that, just the darkness. Few have been brave enough to try to find it. No one living now."

"Why do people stay here? Why don't they call the authorities? A company of soldiers could catch it or kill it, right?"

"No one will believe them. Do you believe all the ghost stories you've heard? We stay because we live here, and our people have lived here for many, many generations. And, as I said, it hasn't bothered Indian people. It doesn't come for us. Just the whites. Some people say it followed the Swedes and Dutch from the old country, *underground*, to haunt them here as it had there. It's their demon, or they're its natural prey. Some of the whites say it came because of an Indian curse. That's foolishness. But it may have come from their violence. Earth spirits are good if you treat them well. I think this one came because of the murders, the burnings, the lynchings, the thieving that the people of Uppsala committed to get that land. A spirit like that comes in hatred and vengeance. The earth is more alive than most people believe. Some say the people stay in Uppsala because they can't leave. Something holds them: even if they try, they can't quite get out of town. The earth or something in it pulls them back. Like the sinners in Dante's *Inferno*: they get the punishment they ask for because they can't give up their sin."

"I've never heard you talk so much before, Daniel," Polly interjected. She got up to warm up the coffee carafe.

"And you probably never will again," Dan replied.

"That's why they wanted to get rid of you, Hank," Polly said. "First, they don't want anyone else coming in to take away Uppsala from them, as they did from us and the Norsemen, and they probably did have some genuine concern for you. Once the ghost gets a good sight or sniff of you, it won't stop until it has fed."

"Do you believe in it, Polly Cooper?" I asked.

She turned and looked at me, but didn't say anything.

"Best thing you can do, Hank, is get far, far away, just in case," Dan said. Maybe it won't pursue if you leave here. The town has on occasion had strangers come and go. They come in daylight and go before night-fall and never come back. Uppsalans drive them out if fear doesn't. That's the people's doing, not the ghost's, but it doesn't matter. I'm not being inhospitable. But your best chance is to go as fast and as far as you can as soon as you can. Forget you ever saw Uppsala, Wisconsin."

The sound of thunder rolled over the house, growing, redoubling, echoing. Then rain began slowly and then ferociously to pound against the windows.

"Cassie!" I said.

"Yes, let the poor dog in," Polly said.

Cassie stood midway between running for cover elsewhere and throwing herself at the door. She bolted in as soon as Polly opened the door a crack. Dan got a blanket and toweled her dry.

"Sorry about the rain, girl," he said, "but at least you're a little cleaner than you were."

"Hank's not going anywhere today," Polly said. "That's an all-day, all-night rain if ever I've heard one. We don't get many of those around here. Usually they blow through in no more than an hour. But that's a powerful storm."

Cassie settled into a corner away from the windows. We all sat back at the table, and shortly Polly refilled our cups with hot coffee.

"Saw some good work you did outside today, Hank," Dan said.

"Good guests appreciate good hospitality," I replied.

The sky had grown black, even though the time wasn't much past mid-afternoon.

Then a thought struck me, and my blood ran cold.

"I've got to go. And now."

"Are you crazy?" Dan asked. "No one could get anywhere in that weather."

"I have to. Now, before it's too late." I looked around for my coat and hat.

"You're worried that . . ." Polly began.

I nodded.

"Hank, you just sit back down," she said. "There's no way we're letting you go anywhere."

"We put you in the study in the middle of the house for a reason, Hank," Dan said. "Away from doors and windows you're probably safe. We've never seen anything this far south of Uppsala. Remember: the ghost hasn't attacked Indians."

"So far. But you mentioned scent, and even if it can't see me, my scent must be all over your property. That may draw it where otherwise it would leave you alone. When I was working, I thought I was helping you. I don't want to bring harm to this house."

"Don't worry, Hank. We know what to do. Remember how you spilled lime in the barn? When the rain stops, I'll burn some sage outside all around the house. If it eases a bit, I'll spread some manure— we've got a horse and a cow in the little barn out back. If it keeps raining as it is, the water will wash away any scent."

"I can't be the cause of any trouble here. You two are the only friends I've had in a very long time."

"What are friends for, Hank? You find the couch in the study comfortable? Good. You can use it again. I'll get a couple bigger candles so you can read if you want to. If the rain's gone by tomorrow, I'll borrow a horse from my cousin, and we'll ride well west of here. Don't stop in the first town west: Horton. Did anyone tell you about that in Uppsala? I guess they wouldn't. Folk there won't admit strangers at all. They keep watch. They're afraid of everyone: Easterners, Westerners, Indians, unionists, communists, fascists, Minnesotans, college graduates—everyone. I've heard that some they've driven out, threatening to tar them, some they've beaten and left on the railroad tracks, and some they've just shot. It's partly the general state of things, but rumor is they've heard of old Chookalo, and they don't want anyone from Uppsala bringing it into their town."

So I stayed another night. We talked for a while before everyone turned in. I read a good bit of *A Tale of Two Cities* before I fell asleep. "It was the best of times; it was the worst of times": I'd sure like to see some of those best of times. "It is a far, far better thing I do than I have ever done"—that line gave me something to think about.

Since I'd already read Dickens, I shuffled through some other books: *The Great Gatsby, The Sun Also Rises, Uncle Tom's Cabin*. I turned up a volume called *The Sagas of Iceland*. Dan and Polly certainly had an interesting little library. Most of it was commentary rather than original text. One section caught my eye. Something about the title appealed to me: *Volsungasaga*, the story of Volsung, his ancestors and descendants. Violent, with feud after feud, plus a good deal of magic and divine intervention. It was all compelling, but the story of Sigurd particularly grabbed my attention, how he was lured into killing the man-dragon by Regin, who was hoping to get the treasure for which he and his brother had killed their father. Then I read about Grettir and Glam, the hero and the revenant—that one made me shiver, as it struck close to home. An acorn of idea took its first tiny root in my thoughts. I heard thunder off and on all night. Finally I put out the candles and slept fitfully.

In the morning the rain had eased, but it hadn't gone. The ground ran with dozens of rivulets, and the sky looked like a piece of slate stretching in all directions. The air wasn't cold enough for snow, but it chilled to the bone.

Over breakfast Dan told me the story of the McBride brothers and a number of others about Uppsala, its land and its people. The settlers had thought it prime farmland, but most of that lay to the south and the east and well off to the west. Dan's grandfather had a run-in with the Uppsalans, and rather than try to deal with them, he had just moved here, land that he liked better anyway, and built the farm. Old McGrath had come here before the McBrides. His grandson, Robert, insisted that the ghost had eaten his grandfather whole right out in the middle of the road. He claimed to have seen it happen. Rob McGrath was one of the few adults to escape Uppsala—a few children had done so, sent away in secret by their parents, but not many adults. Rob had tried to get the Uppsalans to give the land back to the Indians: he believed the land was theirs. The others told him he was just too afraid to stand up for what his people had got for him with their own sweat and courage. Well, Old McGrath had shown that courage. He had stood right out in the main road into town with nothing and no one but his gun and two well-trained hunting dogs. His family and friends had tried to persuade him to get inside before dark, but he had shooed them off.

For the longest time nothing happened. McGrath must have begun to think he had scared off the ghost. But about midnight anyone who was near enough, however well housed and well hidden, had heard that wail, coming from a hollow over the hill to the north. The wail got louder and louder, echoing through the woods, seeming once to come from the east, once from the south, once from the west.

Rob, terrified, claimed to have peeked out the window to see his grandfather standing still in the road. The dogs were silent beyond a whimper, flat on their bellies, and Old McGrath, still as a statue, didn't even manage to raise his gun. Something bright white hit him fast as lightning, and three images disappeared in a burst of flame. Rob himself fell to the floor of his house as the ghost ran through the streets of the town, its triumphant wail echoing off the sky.

Nothing was left of Old McGrath or the dogs or the gun, and three other Uppsalans, older folk, had died in the night of sheer terror.

For the next three nights Wiskalo Chookalo had prowled the streets of Uppsala, screeching its wild siren wail, as all the living residents quailed in their homes, afraid to lift eye or ear. They begged and prayed to whatever God they believed in that the ghost would spare them.

"Even that didn't change them," Dan said. "Once the nights quieted down, they were just as mean and acquisitive as they'd been. Even Ebenezer Scrooge could change. Not those people."

By early afternoon the rain had stopped. A patchwork of clouds still hid the sun, but the air warmed a bit. I helped Dan mend a leak in the roof. We sat on the back step drinking cool water.

"I think we still have time today, Hank. I can ride over and get my brother's horse. You may be in time to hop the train, but I can do better by you if we ride west two or three towns down. I can drop you there with some food, get my cousin's horse back, and get home before dark, long as the ground's not too soggy."

I didn't reply right away.

"I don't think I like what you're thinking," Dan said.

"I do," Polly said, coming out the door.

"If he even tries to go back, the Uppsalans will probably kill him. And if they don't, how do you kill a ghost?"

"Maybe you don't," Polly said. "But if you want to try, you need to think about how the world has changed since the Great War. Maybe there's a way now that wasn't possible before."

"The war taught us a lot about killing," I said, "and I'm not sure killing's the answer. From what folks have told me, the Uppsalans have tried and done enough of that already."

"Foolishness. Pure, foolish waste of a good man."

"So you do believe after all," Polly said. "Somebody has to try, Dan. It's been a long while since anyone did. I have a feeling about Hank. He has a plan."

"Why do you think that?" I asked.

She gave me a look that said "don't be stupid."

"I have a plan, too," she said, "and I think it can work. If we're brave enough."

"We?" I asked, sure of one thing: I didn't want to get anyone else involved in my trouble.

FOUR

Of Earth, Fire, and Root Vegetables

"So you're set on staying? What about that aunt in Duluth who's expecting you?"

"She knows I'm on the rails and on foot. Traveling that way takes time."

"You don't have any stake here. It isn't safe, and it isn't sensible," Dan said.

"Neither was signing up in Canada to go to France in 1917."

Dan had to admit that was right. "Or in '15, either. You can stay here, but that won't help you fight . . ." He didn't want to say that name outside in the open air.

"I'm also not convinced that I don't pose a danger to you," Hank said, "though fighting isn't part of the plan. And I don't want to get Polly Cooper involved."

"That's not up to you or me. She makes her own decisions."

"If she's your younger sister, can't you tell her not to?"

"Step-sister, and you've forgotten that Oneida are matrilineal: I'm older, but she outranks me. I can counsel, but not order. But I can ask you, a guest and a friend, not to encourage her."

"Right." *I can't tell you how good it felt to have someone call me* friend.

We were walking south and east to a collection of small houses—more a hamlet than a town—where a number of Dan and Polly's family and friends lived. We went among oak and maple woods, up a gentle rise, then down into a glen. A stream ran through the middle of it. Some buildings sat down along the stream and others on the rise beyond. A dirt road ran into it from the east, but not on through.

"They keep quarters both higher up and lower down, and they use one or the other depending on the weather," Dan explained. There also looked to be a couple barns, a stable, a stand-alone kitchen, an icehouse and a smokehouse, and some kind of meeting hall. Above and below were a couple longhouses as well as frame-and-stone houses like the one where Dan and Polly lived, but not as big.

"It's not a *rez*—reservation, that is. It belongs to these families as their own private property that they have always had and that they want to keep. Fields for corn, beans, and squash over there," Dan said, pointing. I saw a few cows, a goat, and what looked like a buffalo. "The whites haven't bothered us for a number of years, but we keep lookouts anyway. Did you see the one we passed?"

"Teenager maybe, sitting well up in a maple tree? He sat so still I nearly missed him."

Dan made his laughing sound. At first I hadn't known quite what it was or what it meant, but I was getting to like it: understated, but honest. "Still soldiers," he said.

Two women were walking into the meetinghouse, and three men were standing by the smokehouse. Dan led me toward them. Cassie the dog had followed us so far, but she sat down and stayed on the ridge above as we descended.

"Don, this is the man I told you about, Hank Peck. Hank, meet Don Doxtator, Michael Smith, and Bear Jensen." They didn't shake hands, so I nodded to each as Dan said their names, apparently in order from oldest to youngest. The third name surprised me: a stereotypically Indian given name and a Nordic surname. He looked to be early to mid-twenties and was tall and stout with shoulders broad as a doorway, a wide forehead, and a deep cranium. "*Bear*'s a nickname," Dan added, "for obvious reasons." I had thought I had a pretty good poker face, but both Dan and Polly seemed to be able to read my mind.

"You'll want to see Danielle," the eldest man said. "She's waiting for you in the meetinghouse."

Dan nodded and turned that way with no further words. The three men followed with leisurely steps a few paces behind.

The meetinghouse, square in shape and largely unadorned, was made of large logs. The roof rose slowly to a point. Over the door sat a large set of antlers, sweeping wide each way, with fourteen points.

Dan stopped briefly and bowed his head, then went in, so I did the same.

Inside there was a wide space in the middle leading to a dais in front. Along the sides of the single room stood long wooden tables and many chairs. On the dais in front sat three women, the two I had seen walking in and another, very stately looking, sitting in the middle.

"Welcome, Dan, and welcome, Hank Peck," she said.

I nodded my head in a simple bow, not knowing what to say.

"We've come for your advice, Danielle," Dan said. "You're still the wisest human being I know." He smiled, and his eyes beamed. She sat stoically, almost without expression, though she fixed her eyes on me for some time.

The three men I had met outside joined the women in the front of the hall.

"I'm Danielle Doxtator. I understand you've seen something unusual: an *ohsúhtok*."

"I don't know for sure what I saw, ma'am, but I appreciate your talking with me, and I'll be glad for any advice you can offer."

"The best thing you can do is to leave this place. Get as far away as you can. If you did see an *ohsúhtok*, it has nothing to do with you— unless you insist on not leaving it alone." I didn't say anything, and she continued looking me right in the eyes. "I get the impression that you don't intend to leave it alone."

"Do you have some business that brought you here?" Don Doxtator asked.

"None that I know of. I'm just passing through."

"Do you have family or friends?" Danielle asked.

"Not in Uppsala. I believe I now have some friends here, though."

"Do you typically place your friends in danger?"

That hurt. "No, ma'am, I don't. Dan assures me that whatever it is, ghost, monster, or man, it takes no interest in Oneida people, at least not on this side of the railroad. But I feel, deep down, as though I've stirred something up and that I have an obligation to try to settle it, to put whatever it is to rest."

"That's a lot to ask of yourself—or of others. One doesn't simply settle earth spirits."

"Is that what it is, an earth spirit? What does that mean? Is it something immortal that, once it's gotten angry, never gives up or goes away?"

"Do you intend to try to fight it?"

"Fight: I'd rather not. I have another idea taking shape. I'd like to try to get the anger out of that place, out of its people."

"You have the power to take away others' anger?"

"Not normally, but in this case . . ."

"And you want Dan Cornelius and Polly Cooper to help you."

"No, ma'am. I'm not intending to get anyone else involved."

"But you have involved them, if they have become your friends. They won't simply allow you to go out and die alone."

That struck me, too. I didn't want to die alone, but better that than dying with Dan or Polly.

Dan knew I was struggling and spoke up to help me.

"Hank hasn't made a decision yet, and neither have we."

"Will you take my advice if I offer it?" The woman would have made a great military officer. She had a quality of command without ever raising her voice or changing her expression.

I looked at Dan, and he nodded.

"Yes," I said.

She didn't reply immediately. "You both give me a great responsibility by seeking my advice. Human beings must make their own free choices. They should make them taking into account their communities, families, and friends. According to the old ways, the old beliefs, you can't kill spirits like this one. Oh yes, it's a real thing, not a dream or disease of your imagination, but you can't destroy it as you would a man or a mortal beast, like a rabid dog. My advice is the same as it was: go away, far away. If you find yourself unable to take that advice, if your heart speaks to you otherwise, face the spirit with courage and an open heart, with wisdom rather than weapons, alone if you can, or with such friends as your conscience allows you to place in danger of losing their lives."

Dan let out his breath audibly. He must have been holding it while he waited for the wise woman's words.

As for me: part of my heart sank, and part of my spirit rose to a challenge that my soul told me was mine to face.

The three women and three men converged on the dais, where they stood talking quietly for several minutes. Dan remained still and quiet, so I did, too.

From what I could tell, all six of them spoke, and everyone listened carefully to each other. Several times I saw the eldest man shake his head, a little more vigorously each time.

Finally Danielle Doxtator emerged from the group and walked up to Dan and me.

"We have a consensus. This evening we'll hold a gathering. Hank, you may have heard it called *pow wow* among other peoples, but we don't normally use that expression anymore."

"This *evening*?" Dan asked. I thought I had spoken it, since the utterance echoed my thought exactly in tone as well as word. But the woman looked at Dan.

"We have avoided the night for too long. The Creator gave us night as well as day to use as we need them. We'll send right now for the others who live nearby. We will meet as a community, show our united strength, and speak with such spirits as will come to us. We will celebrate the earth and its creatures, and we will seek guidance for Hank Peck as well as for our own people. The council has decided. Everyone get busy. We have a lot to do."

I had heard of pow wows, but had never seen one and had no idea what people did there. I had assumed that white people wouldn't be welcome.

"Well, Hank, you have another adventure ahead of you. Besides the tribal members, friends are sometimes welcomed to a pow wow, but that seldom means white folk. We've had them all along, of course, but not at night, not since events took their course at Uppsala. It's about time we made the night our own again. Come on: they'll need help preparing. I'll need to go for Polly. Bear Jensen will show you what to do."

I'm not a big man. In those days I was about five foot ten, and when I had steady work and food I weighed about a hundred seventy pounds—though the previous couple days were the first time I'd eaten regularly in some time. Bear Jensen had sauntered over next to us. He was a more than a head taller than I was, and he had a large head. I'd guess he had nearly a hundred pounds on me. But his expression was gentle and unthreatening, almost a smile. He made a slight motion with his head toward the door, then went outside. I followed.

Dan began walking back in the direction we'd come. He was up the hill in no time. I saw Cassie rise to meet him, wagging her tail. He patted her on the head as he passed, and she sat back down, looking at me. Even from that distance I could see her eyes glowing.

I followed Bear to one of the barns, where he picked up six chairs, three in each hand. I did the same and followed him back toward the meetinghouse. He managed it more easily than I did. We made two more forays for additional chairs, then began setting up the hall: he spoke no directions, so I just followed his actions.

We collected good wood and kindling for a large fire in the clearing in front of the meetinghouse.

In front of the smokehouse we washed our hands with water we pumped from a well. Inside he took down large chunks of dried meat, venison. He handed me a knife and showed me how he wanted the slices done. A woman arrived with some large serving plates, and we placed the meat on them and carried them back to the hall, too. With such chores we filled most of the rest of the afternoon. We finished by carrying several large loads of leather wraps and animal furs into one of the longhouses.

People who had been there when I arrived had changed into ceremonial dress of leather and fur, decorated with beads, stones, and feathers.

Others, people of all ages, anyone who could walk or whom someone could carry, began to arrive from all different directions, they too costumed for an obviously important event. Someone had just started the bonfire in the clearing. Drummers had set up chairs in a semi-circle around the nascent fire and were testing their rhythms together. In what must have been less than half an hour, the sound settled into a steady pattern and intensified, and chanters joined the drummers in a hypnotic chorus. I couldn't discern any words: just sounds, but sounds that militated against the need for words. The chants resounded though the glen with the ache of living: the sorrows of love and loss, lament for people and lands and creatures gone or ripped away, for the inexorable rush of time that takes our strength and wisdom, for the turning of fall into crushing winter, for the sense that we can never live up to our ancestors' hopes for us. Yet the voices also tore away sadness with shouts of indomitable spirit, with an assertion of the power and value of individual and community life, with willingness to live for and if need die for human passions, for things that we know are true and right and honest and deep.

In the core of my being those sounds battled the demonic wail I'd heard on my first night in Uppsala, Wisconsin. They filled my muscles and sinews with something more powerful than an idea: with a will to act, to find something to do, with a belief that our actions, whether we succeed or fail, have value. And the dancers: I feared to offend by joining them, but as I stood and watched, they filled my blood and my soul with movement, with action, with purpose beyond what reason can tell us, with something at once natural and supernatural, fleeting yet permanent and perfect.

Dusk had begun spreading its gray palms across the sky when Dan and Polly came over the top of the hill and into the glen. They were striking figures in leather and fur decorated with red and blue, with feathers that made them look as if they could take wing and fly over the top of the little valley if they wished. They joined the dance, and the drumming and chanting once again intensified. The dancers and chanters seemed to me not to tire, but to gain energy and strength the longer they continued. After what must have been more than another hour, the chants slowly diminished, and the drums built to a crescendo. With booms that rivaled the thunders of the night storms, they rose to fill out all the space I could see or feel and stopped so suddenly that I felt as if in the silence I had fallen from a cliff into a bottomless hole.

I needed a few minutes to regain my balance and process the silence that drank up those hours of sound and activity and stirred it into medicine to patch the soul wherever it had torn from sadness or anger or cowardice or hatred. A couple of the elders were walking around the fire with smoking sage, allowing its intoxicating earthiness to waft among the participants and spectators. Though I wasn't a smoker, I breathed in the smoke: it scratched and dried my nose and throat, but seemed to scrape away days, years of tumult, uncertainty, and want.

Beyond swaying with the music, I had been standing still for quite a long time. Dan came up beside me and placed a hand on my elbow and directed me toward the meetinghouse. I felt as though I was walking with bouncy, unsteady steps. Inside the meeting place, fires were burning in fireplaces, and candles burned in holders along the walls for the length of the building. The tables were laden with foods of all sorts: the meats Bear and I had cut; fish; baked and raw vegetables; stacks of flatbread and cornbread; root soups and meat and vegetable soups; porridges; large bowls of wild rice; great crocks of water flavored lightly with herbs or fruit. Everyone settled down to eat, some talking quietly with one another as they all rebuilt the bodily strength they had spent on the dances.

When everyone had eaten, all the people moved toward the front of the hall and settled down there in silence. One by one, the elders rose, walked to the very front, and told stories. They told of the Oneida people, of their lives out east and of their migration west and north. They told of battles, of families, of love stories, of helping the European settlers and then facing their inexplicable rejection. They recounted myths and genealogies, stories of magic and humor, of courage and persistence—they repeatedly reminded me of the saga-book I had read in Dan's study, of Norsemen settling Iceland, facing feuds, sailing south and east and even, unbelievably, to the New World. That thing people everywhere have in common: the love of stories of all

74

sorts, especially stories of things their people have accomplished. The need to retell and remember: that drives us to give and receive the pleasure of stories of human beings, good and bad, who have faced adversity, faced one another, faced all the trials of the earth, and survived.

Darkness had fallen heavily, and weariness had got hold of me like an irrepressible claw, yet I willingly gave in to it. Ghost or no, they filed out of the hall and danced and chanted around the still-roaring fire—this time the dance said, "Come what may. We are here. We accept you, and we will not fear you." I watched Polly Cooper dancing around the flames with a face focused on hundreds of years of her people's resignation to live in their own way regardless of what the world would say or do.

At last, when I felt that sleep must overtake me even as I stood there, the music and dancing died away. Don Doxtator, the elder man I had met earlier in the day, stood by himself beside the now-dying fire and spoke in a clear, steady voice for everyone to hear. He didn't speak loudly, yet his voice carried, moving among the people like one of the dancers carried along by willpower and raised up by the rhythms of the drums.

"The Creator wills us to live. We don't get to understand why, but the earth, the other creatures, the movements of hills and streams, the waves of time teach us how. Whatever happens, we will love and respect the earth where we live. We will remember to thank the Creator and our ancestors for it and to use their gift respectfully. We will not shy away from evil when we find it. We will not seek it out, but we will face it, recognize it, and overcome it. We will be a people among the many peoples of the earth. We will respect them, and if they refuse to respect us, we will at least always respect ourselves, and we will never fail one another. When hatred rises up from the earth, we will drive it back with our love of that very earth. We will try always to pass as good an earth to our children and our children's children as the one we got from our parents. With courage, with heart, with allegiance to our families and friends, we will live lives worthy of the Creator's gift. We will sing, dance, eat, tell stories, pray together, make children, live fully each day and each night. May the Creator and the Creator's earth bless each child that swims into life, each one past, each living now, each to come."

He began to chant and to dance, not around the embers of the fire, but right where he stood. No one joined his song, but everyone moved with it, swayed with it, drank it in, floated on it like lilting, personal waves of waking on sighing whitecaps of sleep.

I nodded off. Before I could fall, Bear Jensen braced a large hand against my back. I could see his eyes glowing in the near-darkness. He made a small gesture with a turn of his head, pointing toward the longhouse where we had left the skins and furs. Many of the people were drifting that way. Dan fell in beside me, walking.

In the longhouse a number of people were directing guests toward the skins and furs. They found places on the floor that pleased them, and they settled down to sleep.

Without fully realizing what I was doing, weariness had so overcome me, I had found a place for myself near the center of the hall and settled down, a couple of thick skins beneath me and a fur overtop. Dan placed a cup of water beside me.

"You may need that to wash some of the smoke from your throat," he said. He said something else, but I couldn't make it out, as I fell precipitously but with satisfaction into warm, lightless, relaxed sleep.

A mist, swirling, rising. Up from the ground. A blue-white light. Rage, growling. A howl—long, drawn, maddening, piercing . . . uuuuuuUUUUUUUooOOOOWWWW! A man, no, two men: one with a flame thrower and one with a Tommy gun. They open fire now: flames and bullets tear through the air, obscure the swirling, smoky blue shape in a matrix of fire and metal. A dust cloud rises. They stop, laughing. Before they can breathe, a figure streaks from the cloud. It is upon them. They barely have time for the first syllable of a scream. Blood and bone fly like spouts from a relentless wave breaking on a rocky shore.

A dream: I thought I had wakened, but I immediately fell again into the darkness of deep sleep.

Then: a woman tall as a goddess and a deer with huge antlers, walking together—both disappear in shadows.

Another image. I'm standing on a rocky outcrop. Below I hear raging water, and from it rises a thick mist in a gray cloud. Not far away I hear sounds of the sea. Out of the mist I see a figure coming toward me. Tall, broad: a man with long hair, a wicked grin, and a patch over one eye. He is wearing leather trousers, a cloth tunic, tall boots, and a pointed hat. He nods to me. "Wrestle me!" he says, and doesn't wait for an answer. He comes on and grasps me with his hands on both my shoulders. He begins to push me toward the precipice. I grab, too, and push back, but he is too strong for me. "You're doing it wrong!" he says. "You are not strong enough for that! Push from deep inside. Let loose the sea inside you. Release the wave of your will against me. Breathe, you fool! From deep inside. Release the strength of the water and the earth from your feet to your trunk to your arms! You must face an earth spirit! You must use earth and water against it!" I did as he said, and instead of being pushed back, I turned him toward the edge and began to push. We reached the edge, his feet halfway over. He released my shoulders, and he stepped back on his own. He stood in the middle of the air, over the precipice, as if he were floating. He laughed. "Learn and remember!" he said. And he disappeared.

Again I felt myself waking. I pulled myself up on one elbow and looked around the hall. I heard the sound of many people breathing in their sleep. I thought I heard the last echo of a drawn-out wail in the distance, but the impression passed away almost immediately. I lay back down, and before any more thoughts could trouble me, I had fallen back into a dreamless sleep.

When I woke in the morning, I was nearly the only one left in the hall. I heard some children running and playing outside the door. I downed the water that Dan had left for me the night before, but my thoughts were so displaced and vague that I sat for a minute figuring out where I was and what I was doing there.

Polly Cooper was standing outside with a number of other women beside a large pot hanging from a metal frame over a fire.

Rays of sun looked like Greek columns as they spotted the ground, dropping from patches of high, gray-white clouds.

"You're too late for breakfast, Hank Peck, but you're early for lunch.

Come try some of this: it will restore you, if sleep hasn't already done that."

As soon as I shook off the shakiness of sleep and had a few bites of hot porridge from the pot, I felt much better indeed. I thanked Polly and went to help with the few remaining chores, cleaning up and putting away the skins and furs, chairs and tables and implements that had come out for the night before.

I wanted to say something to the Doxtators, but I didn't know what to say. I noticed that folk here, while they eagerly enough thanked God for the bounties of the earth, were a little shyer about thanking one another. I got the sense that they thought that saying "thank you" in some way diminished the gift.

I saw Danielle Doxtator and went to talk with her. A bow seemed too formal, but it was all I could think of, so I offered it.

"Your first Oneida gathering, Hank Peck: what do you think of it?"

I thought for a moment. "Astonishing. In many ways it's simple, doing things that humans do: singing, dancing, eating, talking, sleeping. But it goes deep. It reaches the blood and bones. I won't say I feel younger: I don't think that will ever happen again. But I feel—healthier, saner, grounded. I feel almost fully human again, and I haven't felt that very many times in my life."

She smiled and nodded, and she bowed to me. I don't think that's an Oneida practice, and I don't think she was making fun of my awkwardness. I think she assumed it was proper etiquette for me, wherever I had come from, since I had done it.

"Are you ready to go back to the house?" Dan asked. He and Polly had dressed in their normal clothes, and both had knapsacks. "I wondered if you might have to sleep all day. That sometimes happens to first-timers at a pow wow. It's an experience, isn't it?"

"Sturdy again and ready to walk," I answered. "Anything for me to carry?"

"Here, you can carry this pot of leftover root soup. Someone noticed last night that you really seemed to like it."

"I do indeed."

"Before we go, Don Doxtator wants to talk with you."

78

"Right," I said.

The elder was waiting by the icehouse, which stood at the bottom of the hill on our way out. A cool breeze was blowing from that way, and it helped wake me fully.

"Good-day to you, Mr. Doxtator," I said, taking off my hat and nodding my head slightly. The gesture, bowing, something the Europeans did, but Americans didn't, came from the heart, and it seemed to do more good than harm. When I don't know people's proper customs, I just try to treat them respectfully, and bowing seemed not to make them uncomfortable.

"Just call me Don, Hank. Come over here and sit with me for a moment." He motioned me toward some rough wooden chairs that sat outside the icehouse.

"Dan and Polly Cooper told me about you and the *ohsúhtok*"—he said the last word very quietly. "They believe you have resolved to seek it out."

"I wouldn't yet say *resolved*. Something—something gives me the feeling that I should, that I have some business with it or it with me."

"I'm not about to give you advice—white people are easy with advice, but we Oneidas are not. Did Danielle speak with you this morning?"

"Yes, but she didn't say much."

"Prudent. I shouldn't say much either."

"I'll be glad for whatever you care to tell me, Don. I heard what you said at the fire last night. I know you weren't speaking to me directly, but the speech: it felt like something I very much needed to hear."

"You're right: I didn't say it for you." He paused. "But if it spoke to you, I'm glad. We do well to speak what the spirits urge us to speak. Often they do so for our own good, but sometimes for the good of others, too. I spoke from my heart, yes, but I spoke as they led me. Let me hazard just this advice: avoid rash action. Avoid action driven by hatred. Keep your composure, and go where your heart leads you. You have been a good guest here. I believe you are a good man—be that for yourself as well as for the people around you. Find what you *think* is right and what you *feel* is right. If the *ohsúhtok* had wanted you or us, it could have found us last night. No one around here has been out in the dark for so long and so carelessly for many, many long years. We had quite a celebration—overdue. In joining our celebration you have helped us as well as yourself."

He smiled and offered me his hand warmly. I shook it gladly and thankfully. Again, I think he did it because it was my custom, not his.

Cassie the dog was waiting for us at the top of the hill. "A couple of the boys gave her a good meal last night," Polly said, "and they gave her a blanket to sleep under. She looks to have had a quiet night."

Dan and Polly and I had a good bit to carry, so we needed more than an hour to get back to their house.

"Looks like you'll be staying at least one more night, Hank," Dan said.

"Time we made a firm plan," Polly added.

FIVE

In the Meantime

We were sitting at the kitchen table drinking a juice that Polly had made from crushed fruits and vegetables. No one was saying much—mostly sorting through our experiences of the pow wow. My thoughts were still full of the experiences at Uppsala as well as the dreams I'd had in the longhouse.

"Let's go over what we know. Wiskalo Chookalo doesn't come out every night, even if someone is out and about, though the white people often say it does," Dan said. "That's part of what makes it so dangerous. Just when you think you're safe, you hear that wild wailing, and you're done for."

"And it appears not to bother Original Peoples," Polly said. "When we've had troubles, I don't think they've come from the *tshuhkalo*. They've come from white people or, long years back, from other tribes who were raiding. The ghost doesn't enter into our stories until after that last group of whites pushed out the Uppsala folk and started trying to drive Oneida out of our farms, too. We have other spirit folk in our stories, but not that one."

"Could be that the Norsemen brought it after all," Dan mused.

"If it's not our ghost," Polly said, "we may need to take a different approach to ridding the place of it. The old prayers, the old magic, may not work on it. The Uppsalans say they are Christians, but I wonder if they have ever prayed about it."

"A book I found in your study, Dan, the one about the Icelanders and other Norsemen: do you remember a story about Sigurd and the Volsungs?"

"Oh—yes, I do, Hank, but I hadn't thought of that in years. Got that book when I was at the University. Don't remember anything like old Chookalo in it, though. Hey: what comes to mind now that you've mentioned that book is a story about a hero named Beowulf. You ever heard of him?"

"No."

"I read something about him around the same time I studied the sagas. A hero goes to fight a spirit that comes up out of the swamps at night—in Denmark, I think it was. The people there can't kill it, so he comes in to try to do it for them. Now that I'm thinking of it, it isn't a spirit: it's some kind of man, or man-like creature, that comes from Cain in the Bible, a murder-demon of some sort. Beowulf kills that monster, then kills its mother, and later on kills a dragon."

"Sounds like quite a story. The dragon in the Volsung story got me thinking. Maybe something like what Sigurd did with the dragon could work on this ghost."

"An *ohsúhtok* isn't a dragon, but who knows? What did Sigurd do? I don't remember it."

"He dug a pit in the ground and waited in it. When the dragon over-topped the pit, Sigurd stabbed upward with his sword and cut its belly open. The advantage of surprise: attacking it from its own element."

"Hmmm—we don't even know if the Chookalo has a belly, or if it would come from the direction you expect it to. And someone's tried the pit idea before."

"It must have a belly, Dan," Polly said, "since it eats its victims. And Hank saw what it did to the deer carcass."

"I guess that's right. But you can't kill it with fire or bullets or other human weapons. Why would a sword work?"

The story from more than half a century past, of the McBride brothers and their fire-pit, had got out, and everyone around Uppsala had heard it. Dan told me all of it.

"It doesn't kill so easily, the Chookalo," he added.

"You're both thinking about it wrong," Polly said. "Killing it isn't the answer—right, Hank?"

I wasn't yet sure of that, but what she said *felt* right to me. "That's what I've been thinking."

"Maybe," Dan said. "I've had too much of killing anyway." He was looking out the east window. The sun was shining brightly, and the day looked fine.

"Let me show you something." Dan got up and went to his study. When he returned, he handed me a photograph.

It showed four men in army gear, all standing with their arms across one another's shoulders and smiling. I recognized Dan among them.

"War buddies." It took me back to memories I tried not to think too much about.

"The fella on my right: that's Julius Day. He was an Oneida. Lived in Canada and had joined up a few months before I did in '15. We shipped over to France together. He was the best friend I had there."

I waited. He had more to say.

"The picture was taken outside Ypres in '17. Julius died at Passchendaele two days later. He was shot twice. I got shot, too. They sent us all the way back to a field hospital near Amiens, but he didn't get there in time.

"The tall, redheaded fella on my left is John Glauskus. He was from Poughkeepsie, New York. He made it home from the war. He and I did. We used to write once or twice or year, but I haven't heard from him for the last couple years. The other is George Rodriguez: he came from Mexico originally, and his folks had moved to California. Happy sort of person who got along with everyone. He died at Amiens in '18.

"That was at the same hospital where I convalesced after I got shot. They didn't give us much time to recover in those days. You get shot, Hank?"

"Twice, but not worth mentioning. Barely grazed me. I heard the bullets whiz by, but I was so pumped up to fight that I hardly felt anything. One grazed my leg, but it just felt like a bee sting. One knocked my helmet off and left a little scar on the side of my head, but I'm not sure if that's from the bullet or the helmet."

"We were lucky. I had a good medic, guy named O'Brien, get my bullet right out of me, and he poured Irish whisky over it to clean the wound. I always say that's the only time in my life I've ever used spirits.

"George wasn't so lucky. He took one right in the head and went down so fast that I couldn't believe he'd been standing right next to me two seconds before."

Dan handed me a second photograph.

It showed a woman, maybe late twenties, dark hair, pretty, in a nurse's uniform.

"Marie. She called herself 'Marie de France,' after the medieval author—said she was her favorite poet. Spoke excellent English and Spanish, too. Her voice always reminded me of birds singing at dusk, just before night falls, kind of low and mournful.

"Her first husband had been killed early in the war, so she signed up as a nurse and volunteered for duty as close to the front as she could get. We met at that field hospital. She tended my wound and brought medicine, and she always asked me to tell stories from back home. She had never met a 'real American Indian' before. She was a few years older than I was. Her face looked very young, but the look in her eyes was very, very old, aware of all the good and bad in the world.

"We fell in love and got married right there at the hospital. Marie, if that was even her real name, was a Catholic, so we were married by a French priest who was the attending chaplain at the hospital. We had a few really good hours together, when I could get back from the front and she could get off work.

"One day when I was walking back from the front, a shell hit the hospital. Hit it straight on. I could see it from about two hundred yards off. The whole thing went up in flames. Nobody survived it. I shipped home alone a couple weeks after Armistice Day."

Polly squeezed Dan's shoulder, took a basket and went outside to pick herbs. I handed Dan the photograph, and he took both of them with him back toward the middle of the house. I needed something to do, so I started cleaning up the cups and plates and then chopped some root vegetables into small cubes and put them in a crock.

Someone knocked gently on the back door, so I opened it.

"Hello—Hank, Hank Peck, right?"

It was Michael Smith from the Oneida village.

"Your father was a blacksmith, right? Mine too—something we have in common besides our love of pow wows. He taught me metal work and carpentry. Dan and Polly around? We all need to talk."

Michael, I learned, was one of the Oneidas who dealt off and on with the people of Uppsala. He didn't fear them, and he treated them that way. They didn't especially like him, but they did business with him, because he brought things they needed. He could get rifles, and he had a saw mill where he'd plane boards for them, and he did better carpentry than anyone else around.

Dan had heard the knock, so he came back into the kitchen, and Polly followed only a few steps behind Michael through the back door. Polly poured him a glass of water, and Michael sat down and took off his hat. He wasted no words.

"Lucas McGrath was killed last night in the woods behind Uppsala. Torn to bits, and there are only a few bits left. So was a friend of his, teenage boy named Robinson. I was there early this morning to do some woodwork, and I heard people talking about it. And they weren't whispering."

"They know what got him?" Dan asked.

Michael Smith gave him an astonished look. "Of course they know what got him. What do you think it was? People heard that sound, and they found next to nothing of that boy. Hank Peck's name came up, too."

"Hank's! What does Hank have to do with it, Michael?" Polly asked.

"They're blaming Hank for getting the ghost riled up."

"Hank was there for one night, and he did no harm," Dan said.

"Someone saw Hank a couple days back walking across the fields going east. So they know he's still around. They think the *ohsúhtok* is looking for him, that it got sight and scent of him, and that it will keep killing until it gets him."

I had already picked up my hat and coat.

"Where are you going, Hank?" Dan asked.

"Uppsala."

"Bad idea," Dan said.

"What do you think, Mr. Smith?"

"Not sure."

"If the Uppsalans are looking for me, I don't want them coming here or to the village. The days are getting shorter, but I still have some hours of daylight."

"They may just shoot you at first sight," Polly warned.

"They may," I said. "Wish I at least had a gun."

"I have one in my pack that you can borrow," Michael offered. "A Smith & Wesson. Shoots true. Tied my horse down at the front fence. Let's go."

"Don't use the gun, even if you take it," Dan warned.

"Right: I don't intend to use it or even wave it around. Do you have a holster, too, Mr. Smith? I think just my wearing it will do the job I want it to do."

"Borrow your horse, Dan?" Michael Smith asked. "Hank can ride it down as far as the railroad, and I'll bring it right back."

"I'll return your gun, Mr. Smith: promise."

"Call me Michael, Hank, and don't worry: I trust you with it."

"I still don't think this is a good idea," Dan said.

"I know. But I don't have any others."

"I have some, if anyone will listen," Polly said.

"I will, Polly Cooper, gladly listen. But I have to do something right now. I hope I'll be back soon."

"You don't even know what you're going to do, Hank," Dan said.

"I'm going to ride to the railroad with Michael, and then I'm going to walk up through the woods into town. Then I'm going to find out what happened. Can you keep Cassie here, please?"

As I went out the door, I turned back to Dan and Polly. "I can't think of anything I can say or do to repay your hospitality. I don't know if I'll get the privilege of seeing you both again. I hope someday I get a chance to return your kindness. If I can't do that for you, I'll try at least to do it for someone else worthy of what you've done for me. Friendship is the greatest gift human beings can give one another. I pledge you mine."

I hadn't ridden much since the war—a little when I was working in Ohio—but that was my second horseback ride since stopping in Uppsala. Despite the uneven ground, we didn't have far to go, the path wasn't bad for someone who knew it as well as Michael obviously did, and I managed well enough.

"I hope the Creator will take care of you, Hank, and I hope you have a plan," Michael said as I dismounted by the railroad tracks.

"I hope so, too. Truth is, not much of a plan, but at least some ideas."

He handed me the gun in its holster. I thanked him, because I was glad to have it. He smiled and touched the brim of his hat. I hopped over the tracks and began the climb to Uppsala, listening to the sound of hooves disappearing into the woods on the other side. What I hadn't noticed was that right after I left Polly and Dan, Cassie the dog had pushed her way out the door and had followed me. I didn't see her until later.

I didn't want to take the main lane or come out on one of the main streets, so I took the tedious path through the woods. I heard some rustling behind me, but when I stopped, it stopped. I guessed at the time that it was a squirrel or just my imagination.

Going through the woods lost me some time, but it got me nearly to the center of town without my getting noticed. I pulled the collar on my coat up around my chin and my hat down over my eyes—I had the same hat and coat as a thousand other men working low-paying labor jobs or riding the rails. I was glad Michael had a shoulder holster for the gun: I could hide it under my coat. Many times I'd thanked Uncle Sam for my light-weight semi-combat boots: they were a better shoe for walking and riding than most rich men had in those days, and they didn't cost much—if a fella had any money at all to pay for them.

A few people were walking here and there in the streets, but not many: I had the advantage that Uppsala looked a lot like a deserted town most of the time. I made for the diner, the only place I knew where I might have something close to a friend.

I walked past once to see if anyone was still inside. A man at the counter was just paying his bill and getting up. I slipped around the closest corner and kept watch. Another break: when he left, he turned in the direction opposite to the one I'd taken. I wedged in as quietly as I could. No one was in the room—Mary must have gone back into the kitchen. I kept my collar up and my hat on and waited. A couple of people walked by the diner, but didn't come in.

Very shortly Mary came through the door carrying a bucket and washcloth in one hand and a broom in the other.

"If you want to order something, sir, you'll need to do it pretty soon. Not long now till closing." She hadn't looked at me, but then she did.

"Do I know you?"

"Nor very well," I said, taking off my hat and shuffling back my coat just far enough that she could get a look at me.

"You! Are you mad! What are you doing here? If you want to live, you should be two hundred miles from here!"

"I wouldn't mind a little toast and coffee, if you have it."

"Toast and coffee! You should have an army with you! You'll be lucky if someone doesn't shoot you on sight, let alone if Wi . . ."

"You're the closest thing I have here to a friend. I'm not asking for much. I just need a place where I can stay quiet and hidden until dark. Then I'm going out."

"Out? Out where?"

"To the woods north of town."

"To the woods! You are mad. You'll be better off if they do shoot you here and save you from . . . Well, hurry, get back in the kitchen before someone . . ."

But someone did come in the door of the diner: two men. They got one look at me and backed right out.

"They'll go and get people, the elders if you're lucky and troublemakers if you're not. You're not safe here now. Here, I'll get you some coffee, and I have a few leftover biscuits from this morning. They'll be a little tough, but wholesome. Look: my brother lives at the north end of town, Number 12 Maple St., right before you reach the woods. What's your name again: Hank?"

"Right, Hank Peck."

"He'll be home—everyone is by this hour. Tell him I sent you, and tell him to hide you if he can. The other men in town don't like to get too close to the woods at night."

"Except for Lucas McGrath and a friend of his named Robinson."

"A couple of poor, stupid boys who wanted to be heroes and didn't know the limits of their own strength. More bravado than good sense. Now come on: there's a back door to the diner. Let's get you out that way. Hurry: no one's safe here at night, especially you!"

Mary needed only a minute to wrap up the biscuits. Then I slipped out the back door into the alleyway behind the diner.

Three men were already waiting for me. They laughed. Several other men were already coming around the corner to join them. One of the men was Nick McGrath.

"You don't got the sense you was born with, boy," he said. We'd both have been better off if he hadn't said *boy*.

Another of the men—I'd never seen him before—said, "You're the cause of the death of Lucas McGrath and Jimmy Robinson. And you're going to pay for that."

"Aren't you fellas worried about the dark?" I asked.

"You certainly got more than the dark to worry about," the second man said, "and this isn't going to take us very long. The sun's just set."

Nick McGrath took a step toward me. He had a whip in his hands.

I'd used a whip in the war for any number of practical purposes, including getting large animals in and out of pens. I could tell by the way he wielded it that Nick had little experience actually striking anything with it.

With his first snap of the whip he was trying to scare me, not hit me, and he didn't retract it properly. I bent over and grabbed the end and wrapped it around my left hand. Nick growled and tugged it back toward him.

I gave a little with his tug, and as soon as he stopped, I yanked back with all my strength and pulled him down flat on flat on his face.

People would do a lot better if they'd just realize: something has to give. Always. A push requires a yield. A tug requires a follow.

When I pulled back, either Nick was going to fall down or he was going to release the whip. I'd rather he had released it: then I'd have had a weapon other than the gun I didn't want to pull.

One man danced toward me from the left with his fists up. He held

89

them like someone who thinks he can box but has never actually done it.

I dropped the whip handle and caught it underneath my left foot. When the man got close enough, I lurched forward and caught him with a jab right on the point of the chin. He went down like a sack of sand.

A couple of the men came toward me from my right with long clubs in their hands. They left me no choice. I pulled my gun and fired it in the air. The sound startled them, and they stepped back.

A man to my left pulled his gun, but something struck him suddenly from behind, and the gun fell from his hand. It was Cassie the dog: that's when I learned she had got out and followed me. Sometimes we have more and better friends than we realize.

Then I heard two rifle shots in close succession. Around the corner to my right came a man holding a rifle in ready position. He scanned all of us with it.

He was Hugh McGrath. I could barely see his face in the growing darkness, but I recognized him.

"Now, men, if anyone has I grudge against this fella, I do. I know you want to blame Hank Peck for what happened to Lucas and Jimmy. I want to do that, too. But I can't. Lucas was my brother, but he was foolhardy. He didn't have to go out to the woods at night, and Jimmy didn't have to go with him. They wanted to be heroes—I guess no one can blame a man for that. Hank didn't kill them. Wiskalo Chookalo did that. Yes, I'm saying the name right here in the dark for everyone to hear. That ghost was here long before Hank came, and he'll be here long after Hank's dead and gone. It's our curse, and we earned it.

"Now everybody listen. All you men: go home before you're the next victim. Not one of us, not ten or a hundred of us are strong enough to kill that ghost. Go home as quickly as you can. Turn off any lamps and be quiet, and hope the Chookalo doesn't get your scent, follow you home, and chew your bones to dust.

"And you, Hank: you're a brave man or a stupid man or both. From personal experience I know you can fight, but we're not talking about a man here. It's some kind of demon, some deep evil out of the earth or hell. If these men here and all the people of Uppsala will take my advice, they won't take you in tonight. They won't give you food or a place to stay. You have a gun, you have a whip, you have your fists, and you have your foolish courage. Go face the ghost in his darkness, and if you're not a Godless man, may He help you now, because you need Him. Now all you double fools: get home. Get home now! And somebody pick up young John Ames and take him with you. I think he's still out cold. Take him home with you and get him out of the streets."

Hugh disappeared around the corner. The other men glanced at one another and at the skies. The last wisps of orange disappeared below the western horizon. "Hurry," one of them said. "We don't want to be out here." Another waved his club at me to try to show me he wasn't afraid of me, thought better of it, grabbed his buddy by the sleeve, and they high-tailed it out of there. The fellow with the gun retrieved it and put it in his pocket. I helped him sling young Ames over his shoulder. In less than a minute everyone was gone except for me, Cassie, and the darkness.

"Psst. Hank Peck!"

A shadow came from around the corner.

"Hurry, Hank! Follow me! Run! I'll explain when we get there."

I wasn't ready to go just yet.

"I'm Clayton Schmidt, Mary's brother. Mary from the diner. Hurry!"

He ran off around the corner, and I followed with Cassie at my heels.

Clayton was young and athletic, and I could tell he wanted to be outside in the dark even less than I did.

The sky had cleared, and the night was crystalline. A cool breeze was swaying just the tops of the trees.

We ran north for about four blocks, until the southern edge of the woods loomed close and large before us. Clayton turned left into the last street, Maple. Cassie stuck right by me, but neither of us had gained on Clayton. He dodged some hedges and leaped over another, then dashed into the front door of a squarish brick and frame house around the middle of the block. I saw no lights in the house, but I didn't wait for a further invitation: I ran right in, too. Cassie just made it in before Clayton slammed the door closed and bolted it.

"Your dog?" he asked, surprised, obviously, that a hobo would have a dog—believe it or not, it happened sometimes.

"Well, yes, I suppose so. More like I'm her person, since she chose me."

He shrugged, not quite understanding, but not minding the dog, either.

The moon, already well up in the sky, shone brightly in the front window. He was about to close the front drape, but he stopped. "Look," he said. "Right across the street."

I could just see in the dark: a house across the street very like the one where I found myself. A drape was pulled aside, and there was just enough ambient light that I could see part of a human figure. The person appeared to wave, and then the drape pulled closed. The house, like all the others on the street that I could see, fell completely dark. The wind had kicked up further, but otherwise an outsider like me, not knowing better, would have thought that town entirely dead. In a way, it was.

"Mary," Clayton said. "She sent me after you, and she got home. Close the drape, please, and come with me. It's not safe to stand by the window."

Clayton lit a candle and led to me to a kitchen in the center of the house. It had no windows, so he lit a couple more candles. "I have a pitcher of milk and some of Mary's oatmeal cookies here—sorry, but that's about all the food I have." He had a large, full plate on a table.

I realized that in the encounter in the alley I'd dropped the biscuits Mary had given me at the diner. "Yes, thank you," I said. "Anything at all is fine."

"Will your dog drink a little milk?"

"Let's find out."

It may sound to you like a bedtime snack for children, but the milk was good—apparently the ghost did no harm to the local milk cows—and so were the oatmeal cookies. Clayton was as hungry as I was, and we sat down and emptied both plate and pitcher.

"I have some fruit juice and some grilled potatoes with spinach, but we'll need something for breakfast. Will you feel comfortable staying here tonight?"

"If you're comfortable with my being here, I'm comfortable staying. Hobos don't expect rooms at the Ritz and seldom get invitations to people's homes."

"You're not a hobo, Mr. Peck. I've heard what you can do, and now I've seen some of it. I wouldn't have let you go it alone with those fellas if you hadn't taken care of them yourself too quickly for me to do anything." He had thrown his coat over his chair. He reached back and pulled a small handgun out of his pocket, handling it gingerly. He held the handle toward me, arched his eyebrows, then returned it to his coat. "I can use it if I need to, but I hate even having it."

"People around here go about well-armed."

"False courage. Not as if the gun would do any good against—you know what. Mostly when they use them, people shoot at or shoot one another, or they practice shooting old cans so they can tell themselves they're prepared."

"Do they see the . . . *ghost* . . . very often?"

"No. I have never seen it. But I've heard it. Hearing it makes me never, ever want to see it."

"You've heard it many times?"

"No—a few times. It seems to come around when something bad, something wrong, happens. It comes after violence or when fear hangs in the air, or when some foolish soul decides to try to kill it. People have always said that it feeds on anger and fear and horror, that those emotions draw it, make it hunger. Are you the kind of man who likes to take chances, Mr. Peck?"

"Not always. I took a great chance in coming to Uppsala tonight. I'm guessing you're not going to show me anything more dangerous than what I've already done myself."

"Follow me, please. I'd like to show you something useful, if I may."

One thing I'll say for Clayton: he was the most polite of the white folk I'd met in and around Uppsala.

We went through a door to the back of the house. The part of the house that I'd seen from the front looked almost exactly square, with a fence surrounding the back. I couldn't have seen then that the back of the house opened into what the people around that time were calling

93

an observation room or sunroom. It had a tall ceiling and many high windows. The back fence stood a little lower on the east side to let in sun, but otherwise it was quite tall. On the north and west sides it must have stood about fifteen feet high. The windows were reinforced with heavy metal bars—they obscured the view somewhat—and the glass was extra thick, but by walking around the room I could get a good view of nearly all of the garden.

And garden it was: deep, set well back from the house, running back nearly to the woods, it had plants and trees of many kinds. Enough moonlight poured into the garden that I could make out shapes and almost colors—at least differences in vibrancies. There was a willow and some apple trees to the north, and a number of tall evergreens that rose above the level of the fence to the west. The garden seemed to me to divide into many little gardens: flowerbeds, walkways raked to look like streams, a taller fountain and a smaller one. I'd heard that the Japanese make small gardens that look like whole villages, or even mountains with valleys, in very small spaces. Clayton's garden looked like a chessboard of many such gardens, each inviting the viewer to saunter in and look around.

"My hobby," he said. "If we lived in a happier place, I'd make gardens like these for other people for my living."

"*We*? Do you have a family?"

"Sadly, no. I meant all of us here in Uppsala. Fewer and fewer people have families here. They're not hopeful enough to marry and have children. Many of the older folks don't live all that long: the presence of the—you know—sucks the life out of them. You're probably wandering why Mary doesn't live in this house, too, or why I don't move over with her to get farther from the woods. I love my garden, and this is our parents' home. About ten years ago Mary got married, and she and her husband bought the house across the street. People here are greedy enough for the most part, but sometimes when they die and their family need to get rid of their homes, they sell pretty cheap. But it's a sad old town, Mr. Peck, that doesn't like happiness. Her husband lived here for about a year and then left her: he couldn't stand the oppressive fear and soul-hunger that haunt this place. On pretense of going to another town for supplies—he was a druggist—he got in his car—he had come to town in a new Model-T—and never came back. He never even sent her a letter. No one's heard anything about him. Maybe the Chook—maybe the ghost got him. I won't say 'good riddance,' since he wasn't such a bad man. Not many strangers could move in here. I just feel bad for Mary. She's a good woman, and she deserved better.

"Look," Clayton continued. "Look how the wind is blowing—seems just now to have kicked up. The ghost seldom comes out on nights like this. You'd think a storm would bring it, but it likes the calm nights, whether summer heat or winter snow. If you're feeling brave, we can sit here and talk and look at the garden. Please, take that chair: it's the most comfortable. And here's a blanket to cover your legs in case you get cold. The air's rather chill tonight."

"We should let Cassie outside for a few minutes."

"Ah, yes, we should. I've never had a dog, so I wouldn't have thought of it."

He threw open two deadbolts and a standard lock to get the door open.

"This town has some pretty nice homes for a ghost town," I said.

"Yes," he said drawing out the answer as if he felt that a dubious honor.

"How do people make a living here?"

"We don't much now. The brickyard's still open but doesn't do much business. The seed mill does some business. There was a cement block factory, but that has all but closed. Hasn't been much commerce in this town for the last twenty years. Used to be three churches full of people every Sunday, even in the bad old days. Now people subsist. The one odd thing is vegetable gardens: they do amazingly well, even in this climate. Did you happen to notice the bank?"

"Yes: pretty modern for a small town. Nice design."

Clayton laughed, and I heard in that laugh a load of bitterness.

"You're not going to like it, but I'll tell you what happened. The banker, Daniel Horne, made a lot of money for himself and a number of the leading citizens by profiteering during the Great War. They invested the town's money and their own in scrap metal and in certain armaments companies—you know, I'm sure, that some of them sold to both sides. Made a killing."

I didn't laugh. He didn't, either.

"I'm not proud of it and can only tell you that our family didn't make a cent from it. Our parents were workers rather than investors." He shook his head. "And there's more to tell. About four years ago in the summer Horne was building a house, closest thing anyone's had around here to a mansion, in a clearing on the hill on the northeast end of town. He'd have employees help him with the labor—for free, of course—and one evening around midsummer he had his mind set on finishing the roof. As the dark fell, one by one all his workers left without saying a word to him. He threatened every one of them, told them they were cowards—unemployed cowards. And he insisted on working, up on that roof, all by himself. It was dark before he could nail the last shingle—people on that side of town could hear the echo of his hammering. Not long after dark, Letty Hend, who lives not far from there, swore she heard two horrible high-pitched screams: a man's, not the ghost's. And then she smelled smoke. And heard one more scream like a wailing siren.

"In the morning, Daniel Horne's mansion-to-be had burned to the ground. I saw the ruin myself: no more than dust and a bit of smoke. All anyone found of him was his gold wedding band and a few knuckle bones. His wife left town and never came back—not many manage to do that. I guess the ghost doesn't like profiteers more than it likes anyone else.

"I got away from Uppsala for a time, you know," Clayton continued. "Went to university and got a degree in biology, specializing in botany. You'd think I'd never have come back. But the disease of this place draws us back against our will. Few, as I told you, have ever left at all, even for schooling, and fewer yet of those have stayed away. Have you ever read any psychology, Mr. Peck? Some say we're drawn to the thing we fear, that we return to our crime scene, that we cling to the horrors of our own childhood and afflict them on others or, repeatedly, back on ourselves. We're one strange species. You fought in the war, Mr. Peck?"

"I did." I let Cassie back in, and she settled down at my feet. I threw the bolts closed.

"Do you talk much about it?"

"A little. Not much."

"War seems to be an exception to what I said before. Many men don't like to talk about their war experience, and if they do, it's with other vets, not civilians. I've never been in war, and, God willing, I never will be. I've heard people—those who have served and those who haven't—say it makes a man out of you. I have a hard time believing that all the male adults in the history of the world who haven't gone to war are therefore not men."

I thought he was going to ask me if I'd ever killed a man. Many people ask that. I usually just walk away, but this time walking away didn't seem like an option. But Clayton didn't ask—again, good manners.

"What did you learn in the war, Mr. Peck? Is that a fair question to ask? I don't want to bore you by doing all the talking."

I had to think about that for a bit.

"I learned to shoot a gun and to use a whip. I learned to drive a car and to ride a horse better than I had, to work with animals and to scrounge for food and shelter. I learned how to love someone I'd never met, someone who wasn't family or neighbor. I learned how hard it can be to learn to kill a man and how hard it can be to remember how *not* to kill a man. I learned how not just to live, but how to be glad for living—I'd forgotten that again until just recently. I learned how to lose a friend and live with it—no, I didn't learn that: I'm still learning it."

I couldn't say more after that.

"Thanks for answering that question, Mr. Peck, and I'm sorry for asking. We see little of the world here. It's even hard to get books. Mary and I share those our parents had, and I brought back a couple boxes of them from university. I'll bet I've read each of those books a half dozen times."

"And what did you learn from those books?"

"I learned to love books. You like books, too?"

"I did two years of college, but didn't finish. Work took me away from it. But I was glad for what I got."

"You have family?"

"An aunt in Duluth, Minnesota. I was headed there when I stopped here."

"An unfortunate accident?"

"Yes. Tell me about your books."

"If you'd like, tell me the kinds of books you like to read, and I'll see if I have anything like that."

We talked into the night until we both fell asleep in the chairs where we sat.

SIX

Wiskalo Chookalo

I awoke with a start.

Needed a few seconds to get my bearings.

Then I realized what a mistake I had made, falling asleep at night in Uppsala, Wisconsin, in an exposed room and allowing someone else to do the same. The wind had calmed.

Cassie the dog was standing by the door whimpering softly and staring out, her hair standing on end.

Ae! AAAAAAoooooo! WAoooooWaoooooWaoooooWaoooWoooOOO WOK!

The wail. And it was close.

Clayton must have been sleeping even more deeply than I was. He awoke just as the wail grew louder. He jumped up from his chair, and his voice hissed.

"Oh, what have I done! Sleeping here! Get inside, hurry, now, now!"

He rushed through the door and motioned for me to follow. I closed it behind him and stood in the sunroom, watching and waiting.

W O O O o o o o o W O O O o o o o o o o W O ! uuuuUUUUUUUYAAAAAAAA!

The sound was coming from the west, and it seemed to me no further away than the other side of the backyard fence.

I put my hand on the doorknob, held it firmly to prevent its turning. Clayton tried to open the door from the other side, but I wouldn't let him.

I have stood and watched enemies armed with machine guns, rifles, flame-throwers and explosives charging toward me with the intention of turning me and all my fellows to dust and ash.

But I have never been so terrified as when I saw a blue-white mist rising beyond that fence, and I saw that creature, ghost or monster, crawl over the fence, half like a cockroach and half like a cougar. It dropped all its weight into the garden, and yet it landed silently.

Through a knot in the wood I could just see on the other side of the fence what looked like a dog, glowing white and spectral, growling and menacing. Another ghost: the dog from the old story of the McBride brothers, still following its killer?

The larger figure stood looking back at the fence, and it let out another horrible howl, longer, louder, dripping with more bitter hatred than anything I had heard yet—apparently ghosts can get angry at other ghosts. The sound echoed like a bomb-siren. I steeled myself to watch. A good thing that I did: I couldn't have moved anyway. It infected me with a mix of terror and fascination that sucked the strength out of my legs.

The spirit stood, surveying the garden and trumpeting its wrath: Uuuuuyaaaauuuuyaaaauuuyaaa, it rumbled. Its eyes, turning from one side to the other, seemed to emit light and flame.

It was moving among the plants and trees, bending over and sniffing. It must have caught Cassie's scent. There was prey—or maybe an enemy—that the Chookalo had met before.

When it emerged from behind a tree, I got a good look at it from the side.

Tall it stood, eight feet high or more. Luminescent, the whole body glowed white, so white that it almost looked blue, like the hottest stars. It had long legs with thin but muscular shanks, long, springy feet, sinewy arms, and clawed hands that looked as broad as ash-can lids. It had a huge head with what looked like cats' ears, but then something else, a second set that hung down past the shoulders, like wilted rabbit ears—no wonder they called it *Chookalo.*

The mouth hung open and the creature panted—does a ghost breathe air? As the bulbous head moved from slightly from side to side,

I saw fangs and grinders, what looked like rows of both, and a tongue that moved around in the mouth and sometimes flicked out like a snake's, testing the air for scent.

Wah, wah, woooWOOW!

Then it turned toward me, and for the first time I faced my enemy eye to eye, though still through thick glass.

The eyes: light flickered out of them like fire. Large round, lidless, unforgiving malevolent eyes, white as could be, with pupils that looked to glow blue, as if they could strike dead anyone who dared look into them with icy-blue fright.

Something inside me told me to run for my life. Something else that knew I had nowhere to run told me that the first hint of morning light would soon rise in the sky.

YOW! YAYAYAYAYAyyyuuuuuuuOOOOOOOW! YOW! YOW! WAAAAAH!

In three leaps toward me the creature hit the windows with its body, feet, and hands splayed out to throw its whole body against its victim. Whatever it was, it had no conscience, it had physical strength, and it kept nothing in reserve once it had entered into battle.

With its first step I had gathered up Cassie in my arms, and I turned my back to the windows. Glass shattered everywhere. But the iron reinforcement bars held. The creature must have had more ferocity than body weight—maybe that's why they called it a ghost.

I had seen the eyes, and yet I could act. I took that for a good sign.

The force of the body blow had broken a window behind me, too. Holding Cassie, I pushed out through the break, and I tossed Cassie over the shorter eastern fence, hoping she would run away to safety. Light, there it was on the horizon: the morning wasn't far off.

I had left my gun in Clayton's kitchen—it wouldn't do any good anyway—but I had wrapped the whip around my belt. I pulled it off and was about to dash for the northern fence and try to scale it. That would take me right toward the creature's element, the woods, but I wanted to lead it away from the house and from the town. I turned back and saw that it had climbed onto the roof of the observation room. It clung on the top and had bent over, looking inside for its prey.

I pulled the whip from my belt, stepped toward it, and sent the whip with a sizzling snap right at the creature's neck.

YOW! Ya Ya YOOOOOOWWWWW!

I had no idea if it could even feel pain, but I had got its attention. Time to run, and I did. I could hear and almost feel the creature jumping down, panting two steps, then one behind me. I snapped the whip up and caught the space between an upright post and the top crosspiece, and, pulling on the crosspiece, I threw myself up and over the fence. I heard a ripping sound, but could do nothing about it. Turned: there it was again, poised on top of the fence like a vulture, its wide, white, burning eyes wild with wrath and hunger.

Wah Wah WOOOOOOOOOOWWWW!

I snapped the whip right toward those eyes. I stood only a short sprint from the woods, but faced the creature, set my feet and took a stance, and stared into those horrible eyes. In my thoughts I said to the creature, Come kill me if you wish. I will give you no fear to feed on. I will give you no hatred. If you eat, you will get a cold meal. And I believe I spoke aloud, calmly, "Come on, then. Come and get me. But I won't go easily." And I whirled the whip above my head.

More suddenly than I had seen it yet move, the creature jerked its face to the east. It shook wildly, and flame shot from its eyes. It looked back at me, this time not merely with anger, but also with a horror of its own.

I had got lucky: the morning was rising clear and bright, and the pale sun had peaked over the eastern horizon.

The creature leaped.

It leaped right over of me, toward the woods. Just at the edge of the trees it turned and once more cast its fiery eyes on me. It seemed to me to dissolve into the earth, and in seconds it was gone. I heard a brief shuffling of leaves, a deep, low, growling, gurgling sound, and then nothing. Nothing but a hint of morning breeze in the trees. The sky shone clear as the day God made it.

Cassie the dog came running around the corner of the fence. She barked as if to chasten me for tossing her over the fence and cheating her out of a battle she thought was hers, too. And then she jumped up into my arms. She licked my face, and if I had been a dog, I'd have licked hers right back.

We hadn't expected battle that night. We didn't win the one we had. But we survived, and often that's better.

My legs were shaking, but I carried Cassie around to the front of Clayton's house.

Clayton was waiting just around the front-east corner of the house with an old-style shotgun in his hands. I looked at him, and looked at the gun.

"Hank, you're alive! And Cassie, too! I don't believe it. I can see you with my own eyes, but I don't believe it! Oh, you're wondering about this thing. It was my father's and grandfather's. More a piece for the historians than to use for anything. But it's loud, and I thought that if there was anything left of you two, I could fire it and maybe scare that thing away from you."

"I'm sorry about the glass in back. I don't have any money, but if we can get new panes, I'll help you replace them."

"Sorry! *I'm* sorry! I let you fall asleep in a glass room at night in Uppsala, Wisconsin, with no proper weapons and no way to shield yourself. Hank, you're a marvel. If I can just stop my body from shaking, I'll make some coffee, and you can tell me what happened. Hey, you don't look so well."

"I'll make the coffee," another voice said. It was Mary, come from across the street. "Come on. Let's all go inside. If anyone here claims not to believe in you-know-what, they'll know better now. It's not that cold, but I'm shivering. Hank, you're white as a—let's get you inside and get something warm into you. Hey: the back of your shirt is torn off completely! And you've got a scratch—it's bleeding."

Once she mentioned it, I could feel the scratch stinging and already itching.

Clinging to Cassie the dog gave me something to think about besides my own shaky legs. Mary put a hand on my elbow to steady me, and Clayton led us back inside. I may be mistaken, but I believe I saw several neighbors peeking out through their windows.

None of this can be real, I thought, as I sat down again at Clayton's kitchen table. He started a fire in the fireplace as Mary heated the coffee and prepared some food. I felt like I had fallen through a magic hole into one of those Norse myths that I had read about in Dan Cornelius's book. What was the famous Lewis Carroll story? *Alice in Wonderland*, that's it: but Uppsala, Wisconsin, was no child's wonderland. It was a nightmare.

Every time I closed my eyes, I saw those blue-white eyes of the Chookalo burning, burning into mine. I had the odd feeling that I would never free myself of those eyes, never be able to sleep again. But then I nearly fell asleep as I sat there.

"Here, Hank: try to eat and drink a little something." Mary handed me a cup of coffee, some warmed potatoes, and a few biscuits. "Biscuits aren't fresh," she said. "I made them yesterday, but they should still taste good. And I'm going to get some of my grandmother's miracle liniment for your back."

I sipped and nibbled absent-mindedly, trying not to close my eyes. "Thank you," I said, finally remembering.

Mary smiled and nodded.

"Do you have a bucket, Clayton?"

"Under the counter, Hank—yes, there."

I got it and went through the door back into the observation room. There was glass everywhere, but I just stepped over it and went through a hole into the garden. I vomited my breakfast into the bucket.

I found a small door in the northwest corner of the fence and went out toward the woods. The air smelled fresh and clean, so I took several deep breaths and then emptied the bucket and cleaned it out by a small pond with leaves and some fern fronds. I washed my hands at a fountain in the garden, then went back inside. I left the bucket there in the observation room to help collect the glass later.

Back in the kitchen Mary gave me fresh food and coffee—they both seemed to know what had happened, but said nothing. I found I could eat a little better then.

"I'll help you with the glass, Clayton."

"Don't worry, Hank. Four of the panes have broken. I have two more

104

in my basement, and Seth Murphy at the hardware and dry goods store has two extras from the batch he brought in when I built the room."

"I'm not too bad with tools."

"Mary and I do pretty well, too. We'll take care of it after you eat and rest a bit."

"And we'll need to think about tonight," I said.

"Tonight?" Mary asked.

"Oh, yes: tonight," Clayton said.

"It will come back," I said.

"Oh!" Mary couldn't stop an exclamation.

"I'm thinking about what to do just in case it has a mind to come here first. But don't worry: I'm going to lead it far away from here. I'm just very sorry I got you two mixed up in this business."

"Hank, everyone in Uppsala is mixed up in it, and we always have been," Mary said.

"But how can you lead it away, Hank?" Clayton asked. "What power can you or anyone else possibly have over that monster?"

"I have no power over it. But it has the power to find me, and I suspect it will use its power to do just that. It knows now that it has an enemy, and that enemy is living and willing to face it. It will find me."

"Hank, as glad as we are to have you here, you must get far, far away, and you must go right now."

I'd heard that warning before.

"I can't go, Clayton. If I go, the ghost will come right back here, where it found me last, and what do you think it will do? I now have an appointment with Wiskalo Chookalo, and I intend to keep it, for worse or for better."

"You've gone mad," Mary said, her eyes blazing.

"You're not the first to tell me that."

"I need to get to the diner," Mary said, "but first: Hank, where did you leave that bucket? I'm going to need it, too. Clayton, clean up that scratch on Hank's back, and get him a fresh shirt—one of Father's old ones should just about fit him. I'll get the liniment."

As I got steadier, I helped Clayton clean up the back room and clear the spaces for new panes. He had cleaned my cut with rubbing alcohol, applied the liniment, and got me a fresh shirt: the nicest I had worn in a very long time. The pain from the cut had nearly passed already, but it was itching fiercely, as if the claws had some kind of special poison.

"The glass will be fine," he said, "and the metal bars held nicely, but I don't know what I'll do about those scratches on the roof. They're deep, and I think I'll have to replace both boards and shingles."

"I'll help you with those tomorrow, even today if we have time."

"If you're alive to do it."

"Yes. Not much good to anyone otherwise."

"That's exactly why you should go away: now."

"I thank you for saying that, but here's something to think about. Do you know anyone who has ever faced the ghost eye to eye and survived it?"

"I don't know anyone, but the stories say that a very few have. They ran, and they hid, and they lived the rest of their lives as haunted men."

"I'm not willing to do that, and I don't want to leave this town as it's been, and maybe even worse off, since the beast hasn't caught this prey. It may do more harm than it has ever done if it goes looking around town for the person who faced up to it and it can't find him. Who knows what damage it may do? I must see this business through to its end."

"Your end, pretty likely."

"Notice you said *likely*, and not *certain*."

"I've already seen you do some things that few other men could do. But even you have your limits, Hank. You can fight a man, but what can you do against something supernatural?"

"Maybe it isn't *super*natural? Maybe it's *natural*, and we need to find nature's way, not our human way, of opposing it?"

"I'm as open-minded as anyone, Hank, but I have no idea what you mean by that. Can you tell me exactly what happened out there this morning?"

"I don't know that I can get it exactly, but I'll tell you what I remember."

I recounted for Clayton the events as best I could recall or describe them, and we mulled over ideas for a time.

"Should we get those panes from the hardware?" I asked.

"Yes. I want to stop first at the diner and talk to Mary. It's right on the way. We should leave Cassie here at the house for now."

I looked at that game little dog: "Stay here, Cassie, and keep watch! We'll be back soon."

She tilted her head and moaned a little, but she sat down and stayed right there.

We walked into the middle of town—I had my whip and gun hidden under my coat just in case. The walk took only a very few minutes, but when we turned onto the main street, a young man almost ran into us as he turned the corner.

"Clayton! I was coming for you. Mary's got trouble at the diner. You'd better hurry."

"Thanks, Len." Clayton looked at me, and we both sprinted the half-block to the door of the diner. "Here," I said to Clayton, "take this." I handed him the pistol.

I threw the door open. There were three burly men standing around a woman who was seated at one of the tables with her back to the door. One was leaning over her and pushing her, though she sat still. Several bystanders lined the walls. Mary was angry, shouting with her hands on her hips.

"Ivan Huggins, you and your bully brothers can just leave her alone, and don't come back to my diner until you've calmed down."

"Step aside, Mary," Ivan said. "This has nothing to do with you—yet."

I recognized one of the men: Galen, the fellow who had tried to push me around before.

"That's him, Florin," Galen said: "the boy I told you about. Had a feeling he'd show up."

The woman sitting at the table turned around. She was Polly Cooper.

"Polly Cooper," I said, "what brings you here?"

"I brought mushrooms and onions for Mary, and I wanted to see you."

"Figures," Ivan said. "Don't know why anyone would want this Injun food anyway, but you could bet that boy would be her friend."

"We don't like Injuns here," Florin said. "We got them out of here a long time ago, and they should stay out."

"I am her friend," I said, "if she'll be kind enough to have me as one, and any food she has is certainly too good for the likes of you."

I wanted to rile him up, and it worked.

"He's mine, Ivan," Galen Huggins said, "and he won't get away from me this time."

He lurched forward and threw a pretty good haymaker that may just have taken me out if it had landed. After what had happened to me that morning, I was surprised I had any fight left in me, but I was angry at what those three empty-headed bullies were doing to Polly and Mary. I ducked the blow and put my knee right into the man's crotch. When his hand came back toward me, I blocked it and followed with a left hook to his jaw just below the ear. He went straight down that time.

"You next?" I asked Ivan.

"Me, no—I just . . ." But I could see he was lying, and he started fumbling in his pocket.

Before he could get to it, I picked up a chair and brought it down on his shoulder and collarbone. He howled, and a knife fell out of his pocket. I kicked it away.

The third brother, Florin, had put his hands up in boxing position. He almost looked like he knew what he was doing.

"Your turn?"

A little smarter, he didn't say anything. He took his time, measured his distance, got a little closer, bobbing his head. He shot a jab at my nose. I brushed it aside with my left hand. He tried another, then followed it with a quick right cross. With some practice he would have made a good amateur boxer. But people with little fighting experience have seldom learned how to duck. I blocked with my right and then dodged. I kicked the inside of his right knee, and he buckled. A left jab to his nose, and he went down, too—not out, but bleeding and harmless.

"You're making a mess of my diner, Hank," Mary said. "Broken chair, and now all this blood. Bet they wouldn't have tried you if they knew you'd faced the Chookalo this morning."

"Chookalo!" Florin spat out through the blood that was covering his face. "You faced Wiskalo Chookalo! No man does that and lives!"

I handed him a napkin to stop the bleeding. "So far, I live," I said, "but no promises for next time."

I heard a sound behind me and turned to see Hugh McGrath with his Winchester pointing right at my heart. I expected something when we got to the diner, but not that.

"I should have just done this before, Hank," he said. "No more chances now. Say your prayers."

Everyone heard the cock of a gun. Clayton was behind Hugh with the Smith & Wesson I had given him pointing right at the back of Hugh's head.

"Put it down, Hugh, now. You and I were almost friends at one time, and I don't think you're a bad fellow at heart. But you're not going to shoot Hank and live one second more to gloat about it. I promise."

Hugh slowly lowered his gun, and before he could change his mind, I grabbed it from him.

"Forgive Clayton, Hugh," I said. "He's a kinder man than I am, and he didn't want to do what he just did. I'd just have shot you, and that would have been a shame, because this town needs you. You're just not very good at choosing your enemies.

"Not so long ago I asked you a question that you didn't want to answer. Now I'm going to ask you only one more before I use this rifle myself. Are you willing to give me one more night here in Uppsala? That's all I'll ask, all I'll need, and all I'll get. One more night in Uppsala, one way or another, and I'll be gone. Promise."

His eyes glowed. They moved back and forth—I could see that he was thinking. He nodded ascent, and I gave him back his rifle. For an instant he looked as though he was going to point it at me again and shoot, but he lowered the barrel and nodded again.

"One more," he said, and he walked out.

Clayton and I shuffled the Huggins brothers toward the door.

Clayton let out his breath loudly and handed me the gun handle first. "That was close," he said. "I've never shot a handgun, and I didn't want my first and only shot to kill a man."

"We don't have an official sheriff in Uppsala," Mary said, "but Hugh thinks of himself as the man with the job."

"We need to talk, Hank Peck," Polly Cooper said.

"We do, Polly Cooper. The first thing I'd like to know is the real reason you're here."

A couple men who had been waiting outside came in and helped the Huggins brothers out. "You'll have to pay damages for these men," one of them said, but he had no conviction in his eyes and didn't worry me. I hoped I hadn't hurt them too badly. Ivan probably had a broken collarbone and Florin a broken nose.

"You should get a doctor for them, if you have one here," I said. "If I had any money, I'd pay the fee for you."

"You other folks," Mary said to the remaining bystanders, "feel welcome to stay or go, as you'd like—coffee's on the house. Clayton and Hank: come over here and sit with Polly Cooper and me at the corner table. Best place we have in here to talk."

"I'll get a pail and mop first," Clayton said, "and clean up the blood. I should get to the hardware store as soon as possible, too—at least that's still open. You three can catch me up when I come back."

I sat down with Polly, and Mary poured coffee for the three of us. Polly was stirring her coffee slowly, and Mary was looking at me and shaking her head.

"I wish people would stop trying to fight with me. Don't they know when a man has had enough of fighting?"

"You're a little too good at it for someone who doesn't like to do it, Hank," Mary said. "Thank God you didn't kill somebody there. Would you really have shot Hugh?"

"Of course not. I just needed him to think I would. And I do: thank God, that is. And I thank Clayton, too. Hugh McGrath would have shot me for sure that time."

"I don't think Clayton would have shot," Mary said. "He's too kind to shoot another person in cold blood. And I'm sure he's glad that he didn't have to find out if he could do it."

"I am, too. Now Polly Cooper: you and I need to talk. Why did you come here? It's a dangerous place for outsiders, as I can tell you."

"But I'm not an outsider, Hank. You are. This place is partly mine, my ancestors' and mine. It's more dangerous for you here than for me."

"Not with men like those Huggins fellas around."

"They wouldn't have hurt me. They wouldn't have been able to."

She said that with such conviction that I believed her. She was sturdy enough, though I couldn't see her holding off three large, armed men determined to harm her. And yet she had a calm confidence that may just have got them to back off rather than doing anything worse than taunting her.

"But you didn't come just to bring mushrooms for Mary or to fight the Huggins brothers."

"No, I didn't. I came for the same reason you did."

I wasn't sure what to say about that. I could see that in some ways Polly had just as good a chance against the creature as I did. Strength for strength, speed for speed, malice for malice, I was no match for it. If I had to resist it by some other means, maybe her means were better than mine.

"What are you thinking of, Polly Cooper?"

"We can defeat it if we work together."

"You have a plan. You told me yesterday that you have a plan."

"And you went ahead without asking me. Mary was telling me you faced the *tshuhkalo* this morning."

I told Polly the story as well as I could.

"You did well," she said. "You were very brave. But you can't subdue it by yourself. That will take three of us."

"Three?"

"Yes: you and I and Cassie."

"We need Cassie, too?"

"Yes."

"Why do you think your plan will work?"

"At the pow wow, when you were busy with your concerns, I had my own business to take care of. I had a spirit quest of my own to make. That normally requires at least several days, but with the elders' help, I did it in one night."

"Can you tell me about it?"

"Yes, but not here in a public place. We need a quiet, private place to talk."

111

Clayton came in the door of the diner. "I got my windowpanes. Anyone willing to give me a hand?"

"I will," I said.

"So will I," Polly added.

"We'll fix Clayton's windows, and we can talk at his house, if he'll let us. It's right on the edge of the woods. After what happened last night and this morning, I don't think even the people who live nearby will be there now."

"I need to stay here for now," Mary said, "but as soon as Al comes in for his shift, I'll come right over. Count on me for anything I can do to help."

"Thank you, Mary."

She grasped my hand warmly.

"Here, Hank," said Clayton, "you'd better take this." He handed me the Smith & Wesson. "I don't feel comfortable with it."

"I'd be happier not carrying it either," I said. "I'll return it to Michael Smith at first opportunity."

Plans seldom work out as easily as people make them. What's the line from the poet Burns, "The best laid schemes of mice and men gang aft agley"?

When we left the diner, a crowd had gathered in the street. Some of them were carrying rope, and some had clubs—a few carried guns. Their talk made the sound of a low rumble, just as one might hear at the onset of an earthquake, and their faces looked like they had violence on their minds. I had heard of lynchings, but had never seen one and would never see one: I don't understand how any human being can stand by and watch something like that happen to another human being. Hugh McGrath stood with them, but he didn't look happy with what they were telling him.

"Now you folks just let us go," Clayton said firmly and clearly. "I hope you understand: Hank came back to help. He had nothing to do with what happened to Lucas and Jimmy. They took a chance they shouldn't have. If you honor their courage in trying, then so do I, but they shouldn't have gone out on their own. These people here weren't even in town at the time. They bear no guilt for others' mistakes."

"But they brought it out," someone called back. "We hadn't seen it for months until that man came."

"And we wouldn't have it here at all except for the Indian curse!" someone else shouted.

"You have no idea if that's even right, Phyllis," Clayton replied. "Most of us believe the ghost came because of what our ancestors did here. And it may have come regardless of what anyone did. It may have been here for centuries on centuries as far as we know."

"The rest of us don't believe that!" someone else called out—the angry voices were coming from all over the crowd.

"We should hang that Indian right now: she's come to bring us another curse! And we should hang that stranger, too!"

"Do you people even realize what you're saying?" Clayton yelled. "We're Americans! We don't do that kind of thing to one another!"

"We do when we need to!" Another voice . . .

"Hugh, talk some sense into these people. You yourself promised Hank one more day. He's willing to face the ghost for us, to die for us if need be!"

"I tried to talk them out of it, Clayton," Hugh said insincerely, "but they won't listen to me, and I'm not sure I don't agree with them."

"How do we know this Hank and this Indian won't get that ghost after all of us?" The woman Clayton had called Phyllis spoke out again. "Maybe it will come every night and kill us one after another until we're all gone!"

"If you do what you're talking about doing, we deserve it!" Clayton replied. That didn't help: the rumble of voices got angrier and louder. I saw a man near the middle of the crowd point his gun toward Clayton.

I had to do something. I pulled my gun and took a shot in the air. That startled them into silence.

"Listen, please," I said, "before you do something even worse than what your ghost does. I fought in the war with millions of other men so that people won't do this sort of thing to one another anymore. This brave woman has come here to help you. The creature, the Chookalo, is drawn to blood and to fear and to anyone or anything that it takes for an enemy. Any more blood you spill will bring it, and it will return again and again. You can't kill it. You can only leave it alone or make it angry. And right now you're giving it more reasons to get angry. Polly Cooper and I are asking nothing from you but that you let us leave Uppsala on our own terms. One way or another, after tomorrow you will see neither of us again in this town. Agreed?"

I looked at Polly, and she nodded acknowledgment.

"If you wanted to get rid of Wiskalo Chookalo for once and all, you'd treat your neighbors and your strangers kindly. You'd try to make up for anything you've taken from others and any violence you've done them. Violence breeds violence until things get so bad that only war can stop it, until folks get so tired of violence that they simply refuse to commit it anymore. Then they hope that the next generation learns better. Usually they don't. I hope you will."

"You got no room to talk, fella. Why, Clayton, last night Carl Frank, your neighbor, was killed right in his own yard. Torn to bits. What did you or this man or this Indian do to stop that?"

That shook me, and I could tell it shook Clayton, too.

"I didn't know," Clayton said.

"One more death because of this stranger!"

Hugh was laughing sardonically. "Carl was going to kill Hank," Hugh said. "He came over to my house after dark last night. Yes, he was even willing to go out in the dark to do it. Saw you and Hank go into your house, Clayton. He tried to get me to help him, but I said 'no thanks.' His sister found him this morning face down in his backyard with his rifle underneath him. Something—we know what—had torn the clothes and the skin right off his back. There was no blood left on or in him, licked clean by you-know-what—who else could have done it?

"Look, people," Hugh continued, "I'm going to try this one more time. I wish this Hank fella had never come here. But he's here. And he's better with a gun, a whip, and his fists than any of us. Give him his one more night. If he dies—if they die—we're rid of him and one more meddlesome Indian. If by some means he lives through the night, he won't find any hero's welcome here. For myself, I thank him for his war service, though if things had been up to me, we'd have let left the whole thing to the Europeans and let them kill themselves off without wasting one American life. So let's not waste this life: let *him* waste it himself. Maybe he knows something we don't or has something we don't. By tomorrow morning we'll know something, one way or another. Come on, folks. It's a nice day today: sunny and warming up. Winter's ahead. Enjoy the day and let things take their course."

Hugh's speech didn't exactly drip kindness, but it worked. In a few minutes the crowd dispersed.

I nodded him a thank-you. He spat at his feet, turned around, and walked home without another word to me.

Through all that Polly had stood motionless and expressionless. "Let's go," she said. "We have strategies to consider. And we don't have much time."

We went to Clayton's house to talk.

SEVEN

Polly Cooper's Story, and Other Ghosts

When we got to Clayton's house, Polly looked unshaken by what had happened in town.

"Let's get down to business," she said.

"First, let's have some lunch," Clayton said.

As soon as we got inside, Cassie the dog ran up and grabbed my leg with both front paws. "I think we need to feed Cassie, too."

"I think she wants a hug as much as she wants lunch," Clayton said.

As we were eating, the windowpanes arrived from the hardware store. We unloaded them and resumed our meal.

"We should help Clayton fix the sunroom before we go too deeply into planning," I said. "We should get it done before dark. It's some protection at least."

"Right," Polly agreed.

"While we work, will you tell us about yourself, Polly Cooper?" Clayton asked. "I still know next to nothing about you, and I'd really like to know why you're putting your life on the line for the Uppsalans." Then Polly spoke measuredly as we worked.

Polly Cooper descended from the famous Oneida who had helped George Washington and his army at Valley Forge, bringing them food in 1777 when the troops were starving. "The People of the Standing Stone," the Oneidas had a magic of their own: they knew how to survive and hold on to their traditions in the face of violence and upheaval

117

in a world that changed so much and so rapidly that from one generation to the next that no one could recognize it.

Her grandmother on her father's side had been a Wise Woman, training in medicine and spiritual wisdom, and she had been among the leaders of her people in Wisconsin.

Her mother had a stranger story. She was the daughter of a Jewish tailor, Joshua Falk, who had brought his family west with other travelers in a wagon train. He had come all the way from New York and set up shop in Milwaukee, then followed a group of pioneers to a land grant, where they set up a town not far from Uppsala, which was settled at the same time. He had always had a dream of farming on land of his own: what his ancestors had done in Russia before they had been driven out.

Few Jewish settlers had traveled out this way at that time. The family had sent the young Elizabeth Falk, bright and eager to learn, to a progressive school in Chicago, where she had learned Hebrew, Russian, and French in addition to the Latin she had already learned through her early schooling. Moving to the farm with her family, she had grown into her late-teens learning farming and sewing. Their farm was small, and it wasn't on land taken from the Oneida, so when harsh weather and lack of experience had cast the success of the farm in doubt, Oneida people had come to the aid of the family, teaching them to survive on Wisconsin land far from cities, family, and their own traditions.

In those days the situation was no better for Jewish people than for the Original Peoples. When Joshua Falk had gone to Uppsala and Horton, the townsfolk had rushed him out, not even waiting to find out who he was and where he had come from. Elsewhere anyone learning of his heritage had refused him help of any kind, neither selling him raw materials or farm implements nor buying what he'd brought for sale.

One day he'd set off for Madison to try to get what he couldn't get elsewhere. His wife was devoted to him, but after many and difficult travels, she was no longer strong. Before he left, Joshua asked a local man, Ben Cooper, to help Elizabeth run the farm in his absence and to take care of his family. Joshua never returned. The family couldn't find out what had happened, though they knew that of his own volition he would not have failed to come back. Six months later they learned that he had died and been buried in a small town outside Madison.

The local Oneida accepted the young family into their community. Elizabeth, an able linguist, had already begun to learn the Oneida language, and she did her best to fit in to the situation in which she found herself. Needing help and finding herself drawn to Ben Cooper, she accepted his proposal and married him. Elizabeth had a son, Michael, and Polly was born just more than a year later. Her mother knew very soon that they had an unusual child, one with many gifts for learning. Michael was, like his father and his stepfather, good at working with his hands: he acquired skill in smithing and woodworking and farm work. Polly, growing up adept at both traditional and practical crafts, gained expertise in Oneida and Menominee as well as the Hebrew, Russian, French, and Latin her mother taught her and the English in general use by most of the peoples by that time. She didn't get the formal schooling that her mother had, but she learned readily and quickly from anyone who would teach her about languages and cultures.

While Polly and Michael were still young, Ben and Elizabeth adopted Dan Cornelius. Dan's mother had gone back to New York State to take care of sick and aging parents, and his father had died while doing construction work in New York City. Dan kept his surname to honor his father, but grew up as a member of the Cooper family.

Many of the Oneida had become Christian. Polly learned those beliefs and practices without abandoning her mother's Jewish traditions and while immersing herself in Oneida wisdom of ritual, prayer, medicine, and natural magic. While her knowledge and skills benefitted her community, the studies themselves gave her great pleasure, and she had always believed that they would serve purposes beyond their immediate and obvious use.

"That's how I came to have the dream journey, what some of the peoples call spirit quest, the night of the gathering, the pow wow," she said. "I've always followed the old spiritual exercises just as the young men did, though most of our people have been Christian for some time. That night the idea of celebration meant more to me than singing and dancing and feasting. I needed most to celebrate my own visions and to see more deeply. I have always had the sense that I had difficult tests ahead, spiritual tasks that required learning. That spirit quest confirmed it for me."

"You have had more than one spirit quest?" I asked.

"Yes."

"You have learned from them and acted on them," Clayton said.

"Yes."

"May I ask what you saw two nights ago?" Clayton asked.

"Usually we don't talk about it," Polly answered, "but in this case I think I should."

"You saw the Chookalo—the *atyanlusla*—is that the right word?" I asked.

"Yes."

"Not for the first time."

"No."

"You already had a plan, or part of a plan, in mind before the gathering?"

"Yes."

"But the spirit vision showed you more."

"Yes. As I told you, the dream-vision came on surprisingly quickly. It didn't take days of fasting and prayer, I suppose because I had been thinking about it for so long, and I was ready. Hmmm: you two have got me talking too much."

Clayton asked, "But why do you even care about us? The people of Uppsala have never been kind to you or any of the Oneida—or anyone else, for that matter. We deserve no special good from you, certainly not your risking your life."

"My people come from this place. The people here now are suffering from a ghost—a spirit or demon may be a better way to say it—that inhabits this place. If the people were free of it, they might change, change for the better. If someone, not one of their own, but someone different, could help free them from this burden, could give them back the night as well as the day to live and to celebrate and worship the

Creator, maybe they could find it in their hearts to appreciate if not to welcome others. Maybe they could realize that the earth and the sky are here for all of us equally. I would like to see you have that chance."

"It won't matter," I said. "Some of them—not all—will hate anyone different from themselves. They have done it for so long that they know no other way to think or to live."

"They should have the chance," Polly said. "Isn't that why you're staying, Hank Peck?"

I nodded. "Partly. You can't always take on others' burdens, but sometimes you can help relieve them, for a bit if not for good."

"You take that as your task, Hank Peck? You went to war to help the Europeans. You go to Duluth, Minnesota, for the comfort of your aunt. You face other people's ghosts to help them when they can't help themselves?"

"Not exactly, Polly Cooper. I need a place, and family, and friends, too. If I can help others make their homes better and safer on my way, at least then I've done some good. My Catholic upbringing taught me that I *am* my brother's keeper."

"You're a generous man, Hank," Clayton said, "but what you're doing here is partly for you, too. I can see it in your eyes. You have no family here, no history, no reason to stay. You even have a place to go: to your aunt in Duluth, right? What do you *want* here?"

"Hard to explain. Something left over from the war. Even the soldier who committed nothing that other people would call *crimes* may still have something to get free of. Just like in France, I have fallen into someone else's war. Even in all that horror I found friends there and—I found love. Now I've have found friends here. And I have found an enemy. In battle the soldier must face an enemy: he charges, weapons in his hand, with the intention to kill. He may charge with hatred in his heart or lust for battle or the hope of becoming a hero or simply because he is too afraid to stay where he was and be called a coward instead. I volunteered to go to that war. I knew no better. Here in Uppsala I found an enemy not of my choosing. It chose me, though I knew nothing of it nor had reason to wish it any harm. That galls me. If I could, I'd free the world of such things. But I'm just Hank. I'm not even a hero, nothing more than so many thousands upon thousands of soldiers who were just like me, who needed to get away from something or needed to find something. So many people showed heroism you simply wouldn't believe—otherwise, we'd lose our belief in the potential for a human being to be good. I saw horrors you wouldn't believe. Many a fine soul will walk no more on this earth because of that war and all it did—and I'm still not sure what it was all about, why we fought it. Now I need something: redemption, purgation the Church would say. I need penance, absolution. I need to clean up something and help make it safe. I can't do that where it happened, in Europe. They're headed for something worse yet—I can feel it. Maybe, just maybe I can do it here. Not much of anyone left in Europe will remember me. Probably no one here will remember me. I don't care. I must, by my own choice, try to *do* something that I can call *good*. I would willingly leave that spirit, the creature, alone and unbothered except for something I heard in its mad wail and that I've now seen its eyes: utter remorseless hatred and malice. I will try to stop it or die trying. I've died several times over already. One more time means nothing. You know, I don't know how I can ever sleep again. Those eyes: those glowing demonic eyes. I can look at you two, fellow human beings I will be bold enough to call my friends, and as soon as I close my own eyes, those eyes are before me again, the eyes of the Chookalo, flaming in their desire to kill and devour. I want to put that ghost and its malice to rest."

"Amen," Polly said. "Now let's finally work out that plan, all right?"

"Right. You saw something in your dream-vision, your spirit quest: something that can help? You know something from the past that can illuminate the present?"

"Yes."

Polly recalled the story of the McBride brothers and how they had intended to trap the Chookalo and incinerate it. She had been thinking about that since she realized that I planned to face the ghost, too. Their attempt was wrong headed. It made sense as an especially violent ambush against a mortal enemy, maybe even for an assault against some kinds of malevolent spirits: the thought of infernal flame might scare them off. But the *atyanlusla ohsuhta'so* is a very unusual kind of spirit. A kind of vengeance demon, it feeds on the fears and hatreds of its enemies. The more malicious its victims, the more egregious its pursuit and the more fixedly brutal its attacks: the Chookalo faces hate with even more hate.

"You had a dream, Hank, about the two men who went out to entice the spirit, one with the rifle and one with the—what do you call them?—with the flame thrower? Ghastly device."

"I did."

"I saw your dream. Your dream was part of my spirit quest, too, my own vision. Dan confirmed it for me: he learned from someone in town what had happened to Lucas McGrath and Jimmy Robinson. Your dream, my sharing it with you, made me all the more convinced that you and I should face this ghost together. We need a third, too, someone with a strong animal spirit. I saw that also."

"Cassie!" I said. "Can't the animal spirit be an animal? This dog faced the ghost with me at our first encounter—if she hadn't, the Chookalo probably would have caught and eaten me right then."

"Hard to say," Polly said. "It must have sensed in you a strong enemy, but you are a stranger here. Though you're a white man, you have nothing to do with what others have done here. None of your family have come here before, right? The dog may have led the ghost away, or the ghost may have gone of its own accord: it sensed no local blood in you. I don't know. But it has no love for you. We must think about that, because it will affect how we determine our plan. But I think you're right: an animal, especially one as brave as Cassie, may do as well as a man or woman with a strong guardian-animal spirit. Choosing the right companion may make the difference in the success of our efforts."

"What about me?" Clayton asked. "Can I help? I'm no soldier like Hank, and I'm not as brave or wise as Polly Cooper, but I'm willing, and that must mean something."

Polly smiled—I hadn't seen her do that much—and she reached out and patted Clayton's hand with her palm. "You're kind to offer. You are helping right now. But confronting the spirit isn't your place: you're a citizen of this town. Even as kind one, you're still part of the problem."

Clayton just nodded his head and sighed.

"You saw much more in your vision than what you've told us, Polly Cooper."

"Ah, yes: back to the vision. I think our best plan comes from there. I fell into not a sleep, but a trance. At first I saw only darkness. Then the darkness began to swirl, like a dust devil or a will-of-the-wisp, and a blue-white light untangled itself from the swirl. It led me down a path lined on both sides with tall trees. From that dull light I could just see the path, and I followed it down to a clearing. In the middle of the clearing ran a stream with marshy land and reeds on either side.

"The mist rose into a heavier and heavier fog. From the midst of the fog I heard a low growl that rose in pitch and volume until it became a wail at once so angry, so sorrowful, so painful, and so maliciously vengeful that in my trance I nearly passed out. The place, which had seemed to me quiet, even serene, became suddenly terrifying and deadly.

"I could see something taking shape in the midst of the fog. I didn't need to see it: I knew what it was. And it knew me. It screamed in a piercing, high wail: higher then lower then higher in pitch, until I thought the sound would deafen me and my head would split.

"Then I saw the face. You have seen it. You know it. The eyes, the wild, ruthless eyes of blue-white fire. Then the body emerged: long legs for running, strong arms with great hands that fell down below its knees; fur that seemed to stand up on its head; long ears that hung down and turned restlessly, as if to listen to every little sound a living creature could make.

"I stood there, full of fear then—who could look in those eyes and not fear?—but resolved not to move whether I lived or died. And I kept looking.

"The fact that I looked it in the eyes, that I remained calm, infuriated it. Quick as a breath it ran at me, stretched its claws so that in its vicious grip it could tear me limb from limb, shred me to bits. I did not dodge. If flew straight through me like the tearing north wind on the coldest of days, or like a wave that passes over you but leaves you standing, and in that instant I thought I had died of cold rather than from the fire that burned in its horrible eyes.

"Again it shrieked: angry and frustrated, the beast had missed its prey, since I stood there still, alive, unbelievably alive.

"It stood behind me then, and I turned to face it again. Its wail shook the trees and blew the water, in which it was now standing, right out of its spring.

"I began to pray, to chant: I asked the earth to forgive us poor, weak humans for our greed and our selfishness, for our fear and our violence, our failure to know and care for our mother, our tendency to forget our sisters and brothers, to ignore the Creator and the great, irreplaceable gifts of creation. I prayed with my thoughts and my heart. I prayed with my spirit focused, intent. I let no other thoughts intrude in my prayer. The creature could take me if it would, but the earth would hear and answer my prayer. I felt sure of it.

"Then I saw two other figures, shadows, but separate souls. I stood behind the creature, and one stood beside it to my left, the first partly, not entirely human, but in the shape of a shadow with a steady red light, the second animal, but not entirely animal, in the shape of a pure, white light. They, too, were praying, in their own way but as I did, for the earth to forgive us, for the Creator to remember us, each of us willing to die, only so that the ghost might pass away into the earth that had given it birth even as it had done so for us.

"The spirit stood confused. It didn't know how to confront creatures in prayer, creatures freeing themselves of fear and hatred and obsession with their own lives. It wailed its long call, full of the lightning of wrath and the thunder of violence, but that call trailed off into the night and disappeared.

"Between me and the creature the ground began to spin like a whirlpool, and a crack opened in the earth. The crack spread until it passed under the feet of the spirit. Something—roots, hands, the spirit of Mother Earth—reached out and grasped the spirit, not in anger, but in the acceptance of it as a child of her own, however bloodthirsty and remorseless. The spirit descended and dissolved away into the earth, its wailings eclipsed into silence.

"The shadow opposite glowed red in the darkness. The shadow to the left glowed white. I felt as though I were bathed in a blue glow. The others seemed to me to smile, but sad smiles, smiles that know more pain than joy, smiles that understand the sorrows of the earth. And then in my dream I fainted, and the darkness surrounded me like a womb, warm and caring but as old and quiet as earth.

"I came to my senses, exhausted. The elders heard my dream. We all knew what it means. I am ready to fulfill it."

"I was the dark shadow, and Cassie was the white light," I offered.

"That may be so. I don't know if we have the right to risk Cassie's life."

"It feels true to me, that dream," I said, "but I wish it were more concrete. I'm not a shadow, and I'd like to feel more confident about what to do."

"We can't fight the ghost with physical strength. We can confront it successfully only with composure and spiritual resolve. It has the strength of the earth in its bite and its claws. We must use the strength of the earth and the water and the sky in our minds and in our spirits. We have to find a way to draw it to us on our own terms, so that we surprise it more than it terrifies us.

"An *atyanlusla,* even one in the shape of a *tshukalol,* hasn't *mind* as we do. It has something like instinct. It has tenacity and ferocity because it has only one purpose. What I learned from my vision, the *feelings* in my vision, is that the creature, feeding on fear and hatred past as well as present, lives on desire for blood vengeance. It haunts this place because of what the people here did. It isn't a Norse spirit or a Wisconsin spirit or an Indian spirit. It comes from the raging sorrow of the earth, born of generations of hatred and exploitation of others, of selfish violence for brief personal gain, of disrespect for the place and its peoples, of willingness to kill and burn and torture for even the littlest of material gain and personal pride. It comes from failure to recognize another human to be just as worthy and important and alive as oneself. We fail, generation after generation, to learn the most difficult and most important lesson for a person to grasp: the Creator's wish that we practice compassion or empathy. We say 'Give me more' when we should say 'What may I share with you?'"

Polly paused and laughed. "Listen to me," she said. "I'm sounding just like my brother. My vision confirmed some of the same thoughts

126

I've heard him speak. He'd laugh at me now. I've never spoken so many words at once in my whole life."

We heard a knock at the door.

"Do you need your gun?" Clayton asked me.

"I think if I needed the gun, we wouldn't have heard knocking," I said.

The front door opened, and the sound of two sets of footfalls came our way.

"Mary has a key," Clayton said. "Sounds like her steps. I don't recognize the other steps."

We had only a second to wait. The door swung open, and in came Mary with Dan Cornelius.

"Brother. How did you come here?"

"Walked."

"Dan, I'm very glad to see you," I said. "I hope you didn't run into any trouble in town. We had a bit earlier today."

"They still don't like to have Indians back in *their* town," Polly said.

"Even when those Indians want to save them from themselves," Dan said. "I didn't see a soul until I found Mary here locking up and leaving the diner. The town looks deserted. It's nearly dusk, and everyone must have gone home early. I asked Mary if she knows Hank Peck: she brought me right here. I hope you can use one more person in your plan."

"I saw only three figures in my vision," Polly said.

"Wait a minute," I said. "I had a dream, too—several dreams. In one of them a woman and a deer were walking together."

"My spirit guide," Dan said, "is the deer, the stag."

"I didn't see it," Polly said, "but if Hank did, I believe it. Sometimes wisdom, either understanding or prophecy, comes in pieces, to more than one person at once. Or the third light I saw: it may have been Dan rather than Cassie—neither of us was reckoning on seeing him here.

"Are you ready to face a ghost with us, Dan?"

"As ready as a man can be—ghost, demon, *wiskliyo tshuhkalo*: whatever it may be."

"I've been wondering: what do those words mean?" Clayton asked.

"You'll laugh," I said.

"White Rabbit," Dan said, smiling wryly.

"No," Clayton said.

"Yes," Polly said. "But that spirit is no white rabbit. Hank can tell you that better than anyone."

"Not at all a rabbit," I said, my back still burning with an itch, "but I understand why some people have said it looks like one. It stands mostly upright, but something about the features . . . I've been thinking of it as a ghost, but that's not the right word, either."

"No," Polly said. "*Demon* maybe, but even that's not quite right: I don't think it's something from the Christian understanding of hell. If it's a ghost, it's a ghost of events, a revenant of feelings and massacres and sorrows, not of a person or an animal. It does, though, drag its victims to the earth and consume their bodies: it has physical presence. Apparently it feeds also on their fear and enmity. About human or animal spirits I don't know: I think it should have no power over them."

"I think I saw the ghost of a dog last night," I said.

"Who knows what a ghost really is?" Mary asked. "I've never seen one—as far as I know. Have you ever seen one, Polly Cooper?"

"You folks can talk ghosts," Clayton said. "I have no intention of facing any, but I have an idea that may help. You may need a distraction, and I think I have one for you. Go ahead without me: I'm going downstairs to get something, and I'll be back up in a bit. Make yourselves at home, everyone."

"Hmmm, a ghost," Polly said—"in visions, yes. In person, no. I believe I have seen animal spirits and earth spirits. I have seen figures that seemed to me to have good intentions, evil intentions, or no intentions at all. But no ghosts."

"You have seen a ghost, Hank, I think." Dan spoke in nearly a whisper.

"Yes. Yes, I think I have."

"In the war."

"Yes. In France."

The others sat there listening intently for me to speak.

"We don't have time for this now. We need to make our plan clear and specific."

"Unless you intend to talk all night, Hank Peck, tell us what you saw. It may help us. Good knowing makes for good planning."

"Not an easy story to tell."

"Try," Mary said. "You'll feel better for telling it to friends, and we'll feel better for knowing. No one in this room will pass judgment on you."

"Well then. At the Battle at Passchendaele in 1917, outside Ypres, and again at Ypres: the suffering there was horrible. General Haig had pushed too hard, too far, beyond the endurance of the soldiers and past territory we could reasonably defend—you remember it, Dan."

"I do."

"The Germans used chlorine gas at Ypres in '15 and mustard gas there in '17—the Canadian 1st Army got it bad there. The British used chlorine in '15 at Loos, but wind blew it back onto their own line. Nobody says much about it now, but Allied soldiers fired poisoned-gas shells back at the Germans in '18—I didn't see that, but I heard about it, and I wished that even though the enemy had done it, we hadn't. The evils that we do live after us: where does that line come from?"

"Shakespeare," Dan said. "Can't remember which play—*Julius Caesar*, maybe."

"I got shot at enough and did enough shooting of my own, but I was never in a gas attack—a little luck there, I guess. But one night I was in the trench—the weather was bad, rain, fog, and cold, and nobody could see much—so we just sat against the wall, weapons ready, and waited for orders or for some sound over there to shoot at.

"The trenches were a hell of their own: cold, wet, mucky, murky, full of rats and lice and disease, full of blood that made rivulets in the mud, the screech of shells arcing over and diving in, the slashing skip and pock and whine of random bullets overhead. We'd been out there for so long that, one night, most of the men had dropped off to sleep—not from any fleeting sense of safety, but from sheer exhaustion. My buddy, Fred Gavin, standing right next to me, was the only other person I knew for sure was awake. He was about six feet away, and I couldn't make out his features in the murk. We had waited there for hours for orders.

"For a few minutes I had heard from over the top a scratching sound. At first it hadn't even entered my thoughts. But it persisted, so finally I began to try to listen with some effort. It would stop and start periodically. It was getting a little louder, but not loud enough to cause concern. Just enough to make me notice.

"'You hear anything, Fred?'

"'Like what?'

"'A scratching sound, scraping maybe, over the top and out a bit.'

"'Nobody out there tonight, Hank: you can count on it. Not us or Gerry. Fog's thick as cream and smells of petroleum.'

"I kept listening. The sound would start and stop, start and stop. Fred must have sensed my tension, because I'm sure he couldn't have heard even my breathing.

"'You're skittish tonight, Hank. What's bothering you?'

"'I have a feeling someone's out there, or something.'

"'Probably just a crow or something like that. Don't worry. Here, have a swig of this.'

"Fred had got himself a flask of whisky. It wasn't good whisky, but he was very proud of it, and it meant a lot to him to have it and to share it. I took a drink and offered him some water from my canteen. I was always careful to fill up whenever I had the opportunity, and a lot of fellas who hadn't taken so much care drank from that canteen, too.

"After a sigh at his swallow of whisky, Fred stayed quiet, and I kept listening.

"I heard what sounded like shallow, troubled breathing and then a very weak but human sound: 'hel—help, help me.'

"'You must have heard that, Fred,' I said.

"'Didn't hear a thing," he said, 'except my stomach growling. Wish I could get it to stop doing that. Wouldn't want to draw a German bullet because my stomach growled. Look, Hank, if you're worried about something out there, I'll go get a sergeant or somebody to see if we can take a look.'

"I think there's someone out there. An injured soldier."

"Not likely, and if there is, we probably can't help him. You just stay here, and I'll be right back."

"'All right.'

"Fred disappeared, and in a few seconds I heard the voice again: 'Help me, please. Can't breathe. Can't breathe. Burning. Hel' . . .' The voice sounded English. Not London Cockney, but northern, maybe. I don't know British accents very well.

"That voice sounded terrible, full of pain, and I couldn't get myself to wait for Fred to come back. I slipped my rifle on my back and, as quietly as I could, I went over the top.

"I could see nothing. I slid ahead on my belly, slowly, as quietly as I could, and I kept listening.

"'Help, lad—help me. I'm here, here. Help, please.'

"Something took shape just ahead. 'Coming,' I said. "Hold on."

"A bullet whizzed just above my head, and then another. Somehow they missed both the shape ahead in the darkness and me. I flattened out and waited, trying to breathe without making a sound.

"I reached out and felt something solid and tugged it toward me. It was heavy and took all my strength, as I was on my belly and pulling with my fingers. It appeared to have full battle gear, and I thought I saw a British Army insignia on the shoulder.

"'Gas,' the voice croaked, 'chlorine gas—don' breathe it!'

"We hadn't seen or smelled chemicals, so I assumed he must be raving in his pain.

"I tugged a little harder, and several bullets flew overhead. I thought I heard a curse in German from a long way ahead, but I couldn't tell for sure. Again I waited, breathing, and finally resolved myself to pulling that body into the trench one way or another.

"I inched back and finally felt my foot fall over the opening into the trench. With as great an effort as I could muster, I pulled the body toward the trench. A volley of bullets skipped over like metal raindrops. I tumbled into the trench, and the body fell on top of me.

"'Thank—thank you, mate. Wa' . . . water?"

"I turned the body over so that I could hold the face up. There was no light to speak of, but I had the sense that the eyes glowed with some hint of life. The skin was pocked, puffy and uneven, like a wet road after trucks have run roughshod over it. I took out my canteen and poured water over the lips, then took a quick swig myself. The eyes turned just toward my face.

"'Thank you,' the voice said. 'Kind lad. Though' I was dead out there. Cold, you know. No more water, no: keep i' for yourself. You'll need i'.'

"'Let me get you some help. We have a medic here somewhere. My friend went for help just when I came over after you. Hold on. I can't feel your breath. Hold on.'

"'No, lad. Jus' stay wi' me. The water was good. I want to feel a 'uman 'and.'

"I grasped his hand, but couldn't tell if it squeezed back or not, my own hands were so cold.

"'Kirkby,' he said. 'Lieutenan', Northumbrian Fusiliers.' That's what I thought he said—they say *lev-tenant*—so I gave him my name and unit, too.

"I thought I heard Fred returning with someone: I heard two sets of footfalls.

"'Just hang on,' I said. 'I may have come back into the trench just beyond where I went out, so the medic will have to find us. I'll get some help: they're just over there.'

"The soldier didn't reply. I went a few steps down and found Fred with a medic just behind him.

"'If I know you, Hank, you didn't do what I told you, and you went over to check out that sound.'

"'British soldier. Found him just a few yards out. I think he was gassed, though I don't know how that could have happened. He's alive, but barely. Hurry.'

"Fred and the medic came right behind me.

"I had only gone a few steps from where I left the wounded man, but I couldn't find him in the dark.

"'He was right here,' I said. 'Couldn't have been more than a couple steps.' I kept going along the trench. No soldier.

"'What's wrong with you, Hank? You got shell-shock?'

"'No, I went over the top and found a man, English. I think he said his name was Kirkby.'

"'No British units around here now, Corporal,' the medic said. 'You'd better not be playing some kind of game. We have soldiers with real problems here. If I hear anything more about this, I'll see you both busted.'

"The medic poked his face right up against mine so I could see his aggravation. He gave me a disgusted look and hustled off the way he'd come.

"'I'm not sure what you did and what you saw, Hank,' Fred said, 'but whatever it was, it was stupid.'

"Fred wouldn't talk any more about it. I checked around the trench and found the marks where I'd gone over and where I'd come back. I found scrape marks where either one body or two had rubbed dirt off the floor and wall of the trench. I found no soldier nor anything that he may have dropped or left behind if he had managed to get up and walk away from the spot where I'd left him. The water in my canteen, with which, as I said, I took great care, was down two more swigs beyond where Fred and I had left it.

"It wasn't the scariest, but it was one of the most unsettling experiences I had in the war."

"You never saw or heard any more of that soldier?" Dan asked.

"I don't know. Maybe. A few days after Armistice I was walking around. Soldiers were here and there, walking through the field or hunting through the trenches. I think they were looking for friends— alive or dead—or for items they'd dropped or mementos or things they could sell when they got home: different motivations for different men. I wanted to get some memories out of my head—and to keep some memories in. I've heard that thieves and murderers feel compelled to return to the scene of their crime: I felt that I had to go back over the place again to deal with what I'd seen there. I wanted to know what was real and what wasn't. I know now that we don't ever really know that, but then the idea meant a lot to me. I also wanted to try to find a photo I'd lost: it was the only picture I'd ever had of my mother and father, taken when they were young and first married. I had carried it with me since I'd left Ohio for Texas when I was a boy. I had to try to capture in my thoughts what I needed to think about from the war and to recover the little bit I'd kept of my past—war takes away your belief in who you are. I ended up walking through dusk and into the night. Fortunately for me the sky was pretty clear and the moon was out, so I had some light.

"I found easily enough some of the spots where I'd been posted, including, as nearly as I could tell, the place where I thought I'd seen that British soldier. But I knew finding that photo was practically impossible, especially once I was looking in the dark. Other men had already rifled through anything that was left to find.

"I'd had to bend over closer and closer to the ground to hunt, when suddenly I bumped into someone.

"'Very sorry,' I said, startled.

"'Not at all. My faul', mate. Looking for something I lost: photo-graph of my wife and son. You wouldn't have seen that, would you?' He was English, but I couldn't identify his uniform. He seemed healthy enough and plenty solid, though in the darkness I could just see that the skin of his face looked a little swollen and marked. 'If you find it, let me know, will you?'

"'Certainly,' I said, though I had no idea how I could find that any more than my own.

"'Lost something yourself?' he asked.

"'Yes, a photograph, too: the only one I had of my mother and father.'

"'Huh! Look at all like this?'

"He handed me a photograph. It was hard to see in the dark, and it was a little dirty and the edges had crumpled a bit, but it was the photograph I'd lost.

"'That's it! How did you ever find it?'

"'Stroke of good fortune. And one good turn deserves another.'

"'Thank you.' I said. 'I'll help you look for yours. Have you been looking long? At least the moonlight's some help.' I bent down to search the ground for his photograph.

"He didn't reply for a time, so I looked up, but somehow I'd already lost him. Looked all around, but he had disappeared in the darkness.

I looked for that photograph for probably another hour, then returned to my unit so they wouldn't think I was AWOL."

I shivered but noticed that the itching on my back had disappeared.

"What happened to the picture the soldier found for you?" Mary asked.

"I have it here." I took it from the small, leather wallet that I carried that had almost nothing else in it, and I handed it to Mary. She shook her head in disbelief and shivered, passed the picture to Dan and Polly. "I heard later that there hadn't been a British unit stationed just there in a couple years, but that they had taken a terrible chlorine gas attack in '15. Didn't have time to learn anything more about the man or his unit than what he'd told me."

"Remarkable," Dan said.

"You are no stranger to spirits, nor they to you," Polly remarked. "Maybe that familiarity has drawn the *ohsúhtok* to you or you to it."

"Maybe you were meant to come here," Mary offered.

"I can think of other spirits I'd rather have seen."

"I've been thinking about this whole sequence of events," Dan said. "I don't think the *tshuhkalo* was coming after you. I think it came for the men who shot the deer in the woods, and you got in the way. The smell of the deer's blood drew it from the ground, and it happened to find you instead of them. It perceived you as something different than it had experienced before. It hadn't yet actually attacked you, though it chased Cassie."

"Since then it has stripped a shirt and some skin off my back."

"But it could have done much worse."

"The itching on my back has gone, and I never did have much pain."

"You sure you're not part Oneida?" Dan laughed.

"Only if there are Polish or Irish Oneida."

Clayton lumbered back in carrying a heavy box and a large leather pouch. He unbuckled the box and began laying equipment on the table.

"What are you going to do with that?" Mary asked. "I didn't know that you still have it. Does it even work?"

"Movie camera?" Dan asked.

135

"Projector," Clayton answered.

"What can we do with that?" I asked.

"Has everyone seen the moving pictures? I was thinking about what Polly said about the need for surprise. I have an idea about how to create a distraction."

"How do you happen to have one of those?" I asked.

"I tried to open a cinema in town a few years ago: showings on Friday, Saturday, and Sunday afternoons. Had to close it: nobody came."

He opened the pouch, then pulled out two celluloid tapes on large reels and placed them on the table, too. He opened the kitchen door and went out into the observation room. Coming back in the kitchen, he said, "It's nearly dark. The night should be clear and relatively bright, but it will pass more quickly than we think. If we want to act tonight, we need to make that plan we've been talking about. Going out is already dangerous. We'll need quick thinking and lots of luck. Maybe we should wait another night."

"That's one more night when everyone and everything here faces harm," I said, "and one more than I've been promised."

"I think I know what you have in mind," Polly said to Clayton, "and it may work. But we'll need some things, including animal blood—something we can sacrifice."

"We can't harm any live creature as a sacrifice to a ghost," I said. "Then we'd deserve whatever the Chookalo would do to us."

"Don't look at me," Clayton said. "I seldom eat meat."

"No time to hunt," Dan said.

"No problem," Mary said. "I have a couple steaks and pork chops at the diner. They're iced, so we'll have to warm them without burning off all the blood. I think I can do that."

"Do you have shovels?" Polly asked Clayton.

"I have one. My neighbor had two. I don't think he'd have lent them to me, but he's dead now, God rest his soul. We won't do him any harm by borrowing them."

"Does the Chookalo have a home?" I asked. "Where does it usually come from?"

"It comes up out of the ground," Dan said. "It can come up anywhere."

"Yes," Clayton said, "but if you consider most of the stories, it has sometimes come from the woods to the east or south, and sometimes up the old main lane to the east where Hank saw it, but most often it has come from or returned to the woods to the north—that's where Hank saw it disappear at daybreak. A neighbor who knows the woods told me that once. I think that's as close as anything to its home: the northern woods."

"Is there still a path through the north woods?" Dan asked.

"Used to be," Clayton replied. "But I can think of only one person who would know if it's still there and who would be willing to follow it. He's pretty old now. Mary, you know Ezekiel Grimsson."

"Yes, but, as you said, he's older now. I haven't seen him at the diner in, oh, the last year, and time back he used to come in nearly every day."

"I saw him about two months ago working in his garden. He's the only person around here brave enough to go out at night. I'd see him walking his dog after dark as if he were taking a stroll in some normal town with nothing more to worry him than a mosquito bite. He'd always laugh when anyone would whisper about the ghost. His wife died a few years ago, and he said death didn't scare him nor any creature that could bring it. Said he'd consider a quick death at the hands of an animal spirit a blessing. He's brave enough—if he's willing and able to help us."

"We need to make a lot of noise right in the center of town: something to bring it right there thinking that the whole town has come out warm and ready to eat," Polly said. "We need that meat and blood, too, to draw it. Clayton, have you got anything to start a fire and cover a pit?"

"That didn't work for the McBrides," Dan said.

"I know that, Brother. I'm not thinking as they were thinking. But we may gain an advantage if the *tshuhkalo* senses what it sensed before rather than something different. A predictable enemy makes an easier foe. We want to appear predictable, but have something that it has never faced before, something that can overwhelm it, quench its ferocity before it can get its claws into anyone."

"Do you know what will do that?" Dan asked.

137

"I've been thinking about if for a long time," Polly said. "I think I do know. If anyone doesn't like my idea, we won't try it. But I don't know of anything better, and right now our alternative is to stay where we are and do nothing."

"I'll be back in five minutes," Clayton said. "Start without me. I'm going to try to bring back Ezekiel."

"So here's my idea," Polly said. "To start with, we'll need all our courage and composure, and we'll need to coordinate our movements."

Just after Clayton had gone, we heard a gentle knock at the front door. I answered it. A woman was standing there with a large crock and several other bowls or plates barely balanced in her arms. "I'm Alma Jones," she said, "Mary's next-door neighbor. I thought you might be hungry here."

"Thank you!" She handed me what she'd brought, and I relayed it back to the others, who had come up behind me.

"You're the stranger, aren't you? I thought I heard them call you Hank."

"Yes ma'am, that's right."

She put her hand on my wrist. "I wanted to thank you myself. We needed someone like you here. We—we've all been here so long that we've learned to do nothing to help ourselves. We'd have done more if we were just better people. I wanted to do something—it's not much, I know, but it's some decent food at least. Thank you, Hank, and thank you, Mary, and thanks to your friends as well. I wanted you to know that we're not all bad people here."

"I know that, Mrs. Jones, and thank you very much." I took both her hands in mine. Mary brushed past me and gave her a big hug.

"I'll walk you back over."

We took the food into the kitchen. I think Cassie was the happiest of all of us.

"Remember the story of Abraham from the Bible, in Genesis?" Dan asked. "Didn't he ask God, will you save this town if I can find only ten good people?"

"He might have held out for five," I said.

EIGHT

Ezekiel

"We needed that," Polly Cooper said, "and that was generous of Mrs. Jones, but we'll need more than food. We'll need all our plans to work, and we'll all need to pray with concentration and commitment. Any who can't do that shouldn't go."

Polly had laid out her plan in less than five minutes.

Cassie was sitting in my lap wagging her tail contentedly. We both felt unusually well fed.

"I haven't prayed like that in a long time," Mary said. "Living in this town, I just didn't feel like I could. But now I do. I've been needing a real prayer and a real purpose for a very long time. So does this whole town. They need something to do beyond just keeping what they stole. I'm a latecomer: the Uppsalans let me in because they needed someone to run my uncle's diner when he died. I was never part of the evils they did here. But by staying, I've allowed them, accepted them. Time to change that. So whether I go along or not, I'll be praying with you."

We heard the front door open, and Clayton came right to the kitchen with Ezekiel Grimsson following.

He wasn't a tall man—quite short, in fact, only a little over five feet tall, and I'll bet he didn't weigh more than a hundred and twenty pounds. He looked like he must have been eighty years old, but a strong and active eighty. And he had on his face the biggest smile I'd seen since I'd happened into Uppsala, Wisconsin.

"Hear you folks need a hunter."

"We do," Polly answered.

"Then you got the best one in town, maybe the best one in this part of the state," Ezekiel said. "But let's be clear: I don't shoot nothing! I don't kill nothing! I find things. I know the woods around here better than anyone ever has, at least any white man. No offense to our Oneida friends here."

"You don't see Oneida as outsiders here?" Dan asked.

"I don't. Your people were here first. Then the Swedes and Finns came. That was bad enough, them intruding on things. My folks came with them, the Norsemen, but mine didn't want no part of takin' from other people. Mine just wanted a place to live, a place with woods and hills and rivers that they could share with anyone who wanted to live here in quiet and peace. When the latecomers come in—not you, Miss Mary: you're one of the good ones—the ancestors of the folks who keep this town now, they was worse than the Norsemen. Took over everything from everybody, and they did it with blood. My folk didn't want no part of that. Everyone but Pop and Mama left, either went on west or back to western Pennsylvania. Somehow my folks loved this place so that they couldn't go. Guess I do, too."

"Do you know what we want you to find?" Polly asked.

"I guessed it."

"Are you willing?" Dan asked.

"You want me to find you Wiskalo Chookalo. That's not very hard. Just go out there in the woods, and it'll find you. Not you two, Oneida folk: you could prob'ly stay out there in the woods all night and never ever see it. Any you white folk, especially if you got a dead deer or even a rabbit: just go out and sit anywhere you want, and it'll come to you. Even you, fella: you the stranger everybody's been yakkin' about? There's something about you the Chookalo just don't like. You don't fear it like the other white folk. That makes you strange to it, which will bring it out for you special, and it makes you dangerous, which will get you killed."

"I wouldn't go so far as to say I don't fear it, Mr. Grimsson. The first time I heard that wail, it nearly froze my blood."

"No, you don't fear it like the Uppsalans do. I can see it in your face." Ezekiel looked at my face for what seemed a long while. "You already done it, didn't you? You looked old Chookalo right in the eye! Ha! Not many can do that. I can see that you did it. You'll be lucky if you ever sleep again in this life. You're lucky to be alive at all."

"Can you tell us how to find the paths in the woods?"

"Tell ya'? I'll *show* ya'!"

"You don't mind going out in the dark?"

"I do it often enough. Nobody knows because they don't see me— they won't go out themselves. Wouldn't go into the woods at night by myself just now, though: that's begging for trouble since you stirred it up. Might go with the likes of you, though: two Oneidas and the man who can look ol' Chookalo in the eye and live to tell about it. Hey: why do want to do this?"

"We want to free this place of the spirit that troubles it," Polly said.

"Oh, you can't do that. The trouble is in the people themselves, not in the Chookalo. You can't free them of what's inside them. Only they can do that."

"Maybe we can," Polly said. "Maybe we can do something that will help the people make Uppsala a better place, a decent place to live. Maybe they'll see that they don't have to be the way they are, live the way they do."

"You folks Catholics?"

"I am," I said.

"What's yer name?"

"Hank Peck."

"Then, Hank, you believe your prayers can wash the sins away from other people, that if they's souls in Purgatory, you can pray them out and get them to heaven?"

"I did believe that once. I'm not sure anymore. But prayer can help— and so can the commitment to do something. At least if it's something you believe is good."

"And you think you're doing the right thing, a good thing?"

He looked around at all of us, and we all nodded back.

"So you're not asking me to hurt nothing, just to show you the paths

141

through the woods in the dark when the Chookalo's out. To risk my life so's you can get a close-up look at it."

"That's it," I said, "though I know that's too much to ask anyone."

"How old would you say I am, Hank?"

I wasn't sure why he'd ask that, but I answered anyway. "Seventy years old."

"Seventy! Folks usually say I don't look past sixty. But they're being nice, and so are you. I'll be eighty-two just after the first of the year. I don't see why I shouldn't live to ninety, though now that my wife's gone I don't care if I live longer. You, Mary, and yer brother, you two was among the few who came to her funeral service. I always liked you two."

"So you're in, Mr. Grimsson?"

"Okee dokee."

"Mr. Grimsson, people say the *tshuhkalo* comes mostly from the north woods, almost up as far as the river. Do you know if that's right?" Dan asked.

"I believe it is. Don't hardly ever come from the south. You'd have to make quite a ruckus down that way to get it to come from there. Sometimes from the east and up the old main lane. But if you can say it has a home, its own hole in the ground, it's up northeast through the woods all right."

"That's what we thought, and that's where we need you to guide us—or at least some of us. We have some things to do both to the north and to the south."

"Trying to outfox the old rabbit?"

"We want to get it where it's most confident and then take its confidence away," Dan answered. "And its anger, too."

"What about you, Miss?" Ezekiel looked at Polly. "You got some kind of magical prayer to work on it?"

"Yes."

"I seen old Chookalo probably more than any man living or dead," Ezekiel said. "Never looked it right in the eye, but I seen it. Many have heard it—you can hardly live in this town and not at least have heard it once or twice. But if you're sensible, or so they say, you don't ever want to see it or let it see you." He chuckled. "I wasn't always sensible. Some of the folks used to dare one another to sneak out in the woods to try to catch a glimpse of it. I actually did it!"

"Shall we get started?" I asked, patting Ezekiel on the shoulder.

"One thing I haven't accounted for," Polly said. "I'm not accustomed to using electrical equipment. We need a way to generate electricity right out in the town square, right where Main and Central meet, or below that south." She looked at Clayton.

"My neighbor—at least the man who was my neighbor—has an old Siemens dynamo, but I can't imagine it still works. We've already borrowed some of his stuff, so one more thing won't matter now. We can at least try it."

"I got a better idea," Ezekiel said. "Hank, you ever work with motorcars? You know how to get power out of an engine battery?"

"Yes, I had to do that in the war a couple times at field hospitals. You have to know how to wire it, but it can be done."

"There's a '25 Nash Quad down at the old slaughterhouse—they used to use it for pick-ups and deliveries before they shut the place down. We'd need a can of gas and hope we can git 'er started. Not many o' them vehicles in this town. The young fella who lives two down from Mary used to work there, and he was a whiz with engines. I'll send him after it."

"I've had to do worse. Clayton, if you can find some wire in your neighbor's shed, bring that, too. Anybody think of anything else?" I asked.

"Be sure to get the meat smell off your hands, Mary. We don't want it to follow you," Polly said.

"I'll use gloves and leave them right there with the last pieces of meat."

"Oh, just one more thing," Polly added. "Hank, how fast can you run?"

"I hope it will be fast enough."

"Everyone ready? Everyone know what to do?"

"Ready, Polly Cooper."

"May the Creator bless us if we're right and forgive us if we're wrong," Dan said.

Somebody said "amen"—I don't know who. I was certainly thinking it.

"First thing we need to do," Polly said, "is to get two holes dug deep in the north woods. I can't figure out how we're going to manage that in time and without drawing the *ohsúhtok* there first."

Another knock rumbled the front door, this one louder than the others. Clayton jumped, and Mary uttered a muffled scream.

"I'll go," I said.

"Right behind you."

"Thanks, Dan."

I couldn't see anyone or anything outside the front window. Surely the Chookalo wouldn't knock, and a crowd of people looking for trouble would have been visible from the window. Whoever knocked was standing right by the door.

The knock came again—first tentative, and then harder.

I pulled the door open.

It was Hugh McGrath. He had his rifle, but it was draped over his back.

"Not afraid to be out in the dark, Hugh?"

"I deserved that," he replied. "But look, Hank—this is hard for me to say—I want to do something. To help. I want to help you."

I turned and whispered to Dan, "One more good person?"

"Maybe," Dan whispered back. "People can change."

"I don't know, but it's a hopeful thought." I turned back to Hugh. "What would you like to do, Hugh?"

"Whatever you need me to do. I have a horse tied to tree down at the end of the street. I don't want to leave it there too long: too much like bait. But it's the fastest horse in town. I know you're planning something with the—the ghost. I know you need to do it tonight—that's partly my fault. Can I do something?"

"Have you eaten tonight?"

"Eaten! Well, no."

"Well then come in and have a bit of food. I'll get your horse and bring it around to the backyard. I think you may be able to help indeed."

Polly didn't trust Hugh, but with his horse he gave us something we didn't have before: speed. And with his two hands he gave us someone else to carry things and help handle the labor.

I left Cassie in the observation room in Clayton's house. She growled her displeasure, but it was kinder than leaving her in the kitchen where she felt pent in and safer than bringing her with me, where she'd risk her life to defend me if she got the chance. I dared not look back to see her eyes—I knew she'd want in on what we were doing—but I heard her scratching at the inside of the door to try to get out.

Ezekiel got back from across the street and nodded "yes." We set our plan in motion.

"Right this way," Ezekiel said. "A child could find it, that old path."

Ezekiel led us, Dan, Polly, and me, with Hugh drawing the horse behind him, through the woods to the north. He followed a pretty easy path that went right from the end of Clayton's street straight north. The path twisted and turned a bit, but it was pretty easy to follow: the main thing was our finding it and its taking us quickly where we wanted to go.

As we walked, Ezekial spoke to us calmly and quietly. I would have preferred that we had all kept silent, not drawing up the spirit too soon, but Ezekial knew the place and probably the ghost, too, better than I did, so I didn't want to throw him off.

"These is pretty nice woods. Not like we had in Pennsylvania, though. That's 'Penn's Sylvania,' William Penn's Woods. Not that Penn was all that good a fella. He did some good, and he did some bad. The woods here are scrubby by comparison. Out east there, they have some mag-nificent woods: tall trees, miles and miles of them, with rivers and streams and real hills, not like these little nobs here. My folks came from there, an' we visited more 'n once. Even mountains, if you go south into West Virginia. You ever been there, Hank? Yeah, them's some mountains, ain't they? Funny, though: if you stick around a place, if you don't come to hate it, you can come to love it. Bad things happen in most places. If you can, you need to fix them. If you can't, well, everybody needs to find some place to live, and you just have to do your best to make it your own place, too. This might be my last chance to make Uppsala better. And I'm real glad to have you folks along to do it with. Here, Hank, here: look carefully. This spot is the most difficult to follow and remember. Get it right when you come back, or you'll get lost in the trees and never find your way in time. Man, I'm glad snow didn't come early this year. The trees are still pretty with the leaves all a-color and still on the branches. You can almost see the yellow ones glow in the dark. In a pinch, too, you can follow the line of the maples: lots of maples just along this path here."

I marked the spots that he mentioned as I had marked some others, with some of the tar we had used to fix Clayton's roof. I hoped that what I couldn't see in the dark, maybe I could smell.

We came out at a clearing with a stream, almost a small river, running through it. The moon shone bright, and the night was so clear we could see if it were dusk or almost dawn.

Dan, Polly, and Ezekiel set to digging.

"You sure you can handle it?" I asked.

"Yes," Polly answered.

"You betcha," Ezekiel followed.

Dan just nodded.

"You and your horse ready for a fast ride with an extra rider?"

"Just this once," Hugh said. He actually smiled.

He mounted, and I jumped on the horse just behind him.

"We're going to make some noise now," I said, "but there's no way around it. At least we'll make the noise going south and not coming this way. Quickly as you can, now, Hugh: to the town square!"

The horse kicked up dirt and darted off in a blaze. We got back down the path and into town in no time.

We dismounted at the gazebo in the town square, where Hugh tied his horse.

Clayton had found a wagon in his neighbor's shed, and he and Mary had carried the movie equipment to the square—and he had remembered the wire, too. Fancier than the rest of town, it had decorative lampposts, a central green space with a platform underneath a gazebo, hedges that needed tending and trimming, a well for drinking water, and cobblestone streets leading in each of four directions for at least a block or two beyond. To the south the street, Central Avenue, went a half block and then turned quickly and steeply downhill. That was the direction where we hoped the ghost would come. Just on the south side of the square stood an unfinished World War I memorial wall about ten feet high.

There by the memorial stood a slim young man, looked to be in his twenties, next to the Nash Quad.

"Reg Cormier," he said and offered me his hand. "Can't believe the old Nash started right up. Had a can of gas right by it. All I had to do was bang the solenoid a couple times with a hammer. Tough old beast." He looked at the sky. "Gotta run," he said, and he did.

Mary ran off to the diner to get the meat, and Dan and I hooked the car battery to his movie projector.

"Chaplain or Keystone Cops?" Clayton asked.

"Sorry?"

"I have two films to choose from: a Charlie Chaplain or a Keystone Cops. Which one should I load in?"

"Which is noisier?"

"They're both silents."

"Which has louder music?"

"I can turn the sound up to maximum on either one. I suppose the Keystone Cops film is more frenetic—I'll hook up that one."

In a very short time Clayton said "Ready." Mary came back with her hands full of meat from the diner, thawed as much as she could get it. Hugh took some and hurried a block south and smeared it in the middle of the street. Mary dropped the rest right at the town square. She took off the gloves, which had a little blood on them, and gave them to me.

"You two should go back to Mary's house," I said. "The basement is probably safest. All we need first is to start the car and turn on the projector."

"Here goes," Clayton said. "I sure hope it works."

It did. He needed three tries to start the Nash, and then despite my makeshift wiring, he switched on the projector, pointing it at the wall of the War Memorial. In seconds the image appeared, shining against the Memorial wall, right where Clayton had aimed it. The sound kicked in: wild, silly music to accompany the shenanigans of the feckless Cops chasing their criminals. He switched if off.

"One hour, right?" he said. "It'll get mighty dark in half that time."

"Right. I'll turn it on in an hour and get to my post."

"You be careful, Hank," Mary said. "Run like the wind."

"I will—thank you."

They ran off east. As they turned north, they both waved: I could see them clearly in the moonlight. Having got that far with our plan, I'd have felt better if the sky had clouded over and a nice mist had risen up. I told Hugh what I had in mind for him, and then I began to check the stars for constellations to pass the time.

"Times like this I wish I smoked," Hugh said.

"Why?"

"Give me something to do."

"Why don't you?"

"Never liked the stuff."

"I don't, either."

As the others had taken their posts back in the woods, I waited to take mine: right in the center of town until the picture started, then two blocks east of the central square, so that I could see clearly and so that, if our plan worked, the Chookalo could see me.

I sat down on the platform and tried to prepare for what I needed to do. Hugh had nothing else to do, so he sat down next to me in silence. I realized then that I couldn't remember very many prayers. The "Our Father" and "Ave Maria" didn't seem right to fight a ghost. Then a remembered a Franciscan "peace prayer" that my mother taught me when I was very small. It went like this:

Lord, make me an instrument of your peace.
Where there is hatred, let me sow love.
Where there is injury, pardon;
Where there is discord, union;
Where there is doubt, faith;
Where there is error, truth;
Where there is despair, hope;
Where there is darkness, light;

Where there is sadness, joy.

I thought I had better rehearse it, so I spoke it several times quietly to myself so that I could use it when I needed it. The last time I said it, I must have spoken it aloud.

"A prayer!" Hugh said. "I didn't take you for a praying man, Hank."

"Are you a praying man, Hugh?"

"Hmmph. Never been a praying man. Used to pray as a boy, though. I thought it meant something then."

"Maybe it did."

"Maybe. Can you say that prayer over again?"

I did.

"Once more, maybe: I think I've got some of it."

I did the first couple lines, and, with just a little hesitation, Hugh joined in, and we spoke the rest together: "Where there is injury, pardon. Where there is discord, union. . . ."

When we had finished, I nodded to Hugh. "Ready?"

"Yeah."

He got up and untied the horse from the post.

"I got one more surprise," he said, "and sorry if this doesn't follow your plan." He put on a pair of gloves that he had in his pocket and pulled out a sack from behind the gazebo. He carefully opened the sack and pulled something out.

A dead rabbit.

"Trapped it," he said.

Normally I hate to see animals trapped, but on that occasion I couldn't help smiling ironically. "Take care not to touch it! Drop it two blocks south, and leave the gloves! Make as much noise as you can make. Then back to the square, turn east, and get that horse back to the barn and you into the safest place you can think of. Don't even think of trying anything else. Polly's plan is a good one, much better than I could have done, and nobody wants to see anyone hurt in what happens tonight."

Hugh shivered noticeably. "I think it'll technically be morning soon," he said, "though we've got a good bit of darkness ahead yet. We've been lucky so far.

"Why did you go into the woods, Hank? You didn't do any digging. You could have just come here with Clayton and Mary and saved us a ride and a lot of noise."

"I needed to see the path so I can find it on my way back."

"No," Hugh said, "you did it because you didn't trust me. You wanted to make sure I'd follow through. Can't say I blame you after the way I've treated you. Do you trust me now?"

"You haven't been so bad. I'm a stranger. This is your town, not mine. More important: do you trust me?"

"Ask me in the morning light."

He mounted his horse and began to ride south down Central Avenue.

"You know, Hank, I don't blame you for Lucas' death. That was his own fault."

"Hugh!"

"Yeah, Hank?"

"I trust you."

He smiled, slapped his horse on the flank, and rode down the street. I could see that he was going to have some trouble. The cobblestones, pretty even and smooth as cobblestones go, were a problem for the horse. It couldn't run as fast as I'd have liked until I got to the smoother street a block east. Hugh disappeared over the hill.

I checked the wiring on the car battery. Everything looked ready to go if that battery had enough juice for one more start.

In seconds I heard a noise from down Central Avenue: it was Hugh.

"YeeeEEEEE-HaWWWW! Yeeee-haaawwwww! Yeow, Yeow, Whoop, Whooop!"

I don't know if he was trying to sound like the Chookalo or not.

Then I heard horse's hooves clattering, and there came Hugh riding up over the hill, hollering. He made his turn down Main Street. He never looked back or over. When he hit the smooth road, the rattle of the horse's hooves increased in speed, and Hugh disappeared again down the street to the east. He had done his job. When I was in the Army, the officers had often asked us to do our jobs. They insisted we do what they ordered, no more and no less. Many of the men hated that: we often wanted to do more or less than the officers had asked. I admit: I hated it, too. For the most part I did what they asked. Occasionally I did a little more, like going over the top to find a soldier who had called for help.

I thought I heard a low growling, but I wasn't sure.

Just then I had nothing left to do but flip the switch on the projector, so I did.

Nothing happened.

I switched it back to "off" again, and then again to "on."

Nothing.

Then from the south came a screech that seemed to shake the sky: Chookalo was about, and it must have found the rabbit carcass.

I began checking madly for problems in the connection—I had never used a movie projector before, so I didn't know what else could go wrong. The machine had worked once. I pulled off the back cover, but I couldn't see much in the dark, so I had to feel my way through the inside of the projector. I was starting to sweat when I found a loose wire and just gave it a little push in. It didn't feel secure, but I could do no better without light and tools and more knowledge than I had of how to make a movie projector work.

Then I was sure that a low growling was coming from the south, down Central Avenue, but I still couldn't see anything.

I threw the switch again.

With a whiz and a whir the projector began to move. Clayton had tucked in the reel, and the film began to play.

The silly music of the Keystone Cops kicked up, and the lights began to flash as figures of human beings rushed about on the large, unfinished World War I memorial in the center of Uppsala, Wisconsin.

I had to wonder why anyone liked those films. No real point to them. Just people rushing around trying to evade or catch one another. The sound echoed loudly through the town square.

Anyone who had been sleeping nearby wasn't doing so any longer.

The growling got louder. The music, frenetic and silly as it was, had grown cacophonous.

A shiver went up my spine. I could feel the creature's presence before I could see it.

I turned down the sound on the projector so I could listen.

I heard another sound, louder, one that I had come to know better than I wanted to.

EEEEEEooooooooooooEEEEEEEEooooooooooooEEEEEEEEEooo oooo, WAH!

It stopped, and I could swear I heard sniffing. Then a loud, angry screech. The sound rebounded off the buildings and echoed through the square.

I could just see a blue-white glow rising above the hill just south of the square.

EEEEEEEooooooooooEEEEEEEEoooo Wah Wah Wah YeeeeeeEEEEEEEEAAAAAAA!

The ghost paused just below the crest of the hill. I wonder if it could feel my presence, or if to that creature a human being seemed no more than a fly does to us: annoying and of no earthly consequence.

NINE

Two Reckonings

Waiting for something to appear is just as terrifying as actually seeing it. Yet seeing that ghost, though I had gone to that place to await its coming, I could have waited longer. I could have waited a lifetime.

YAAH! YAAAH! YAAAAAAAAAAHHHH! It screamed again, and there I saw it, rising up over the cobblestone ridge, aflame, shining brighter than a second moon.

The head appeared distended, and flames poured out from the eyes and enveloped the face swollen with rage and hunger.

Part of me felt glad that at least the first part of Polly's plan had worked: we had drawn Wiskalo Chookalo right where we hoped we would, up from the south.

Part of me felt that I had been stupid beyond belief to be willing to face it alone again. I would have been glad to have Cassie there with me, but that would have put her in danger, too, and who could say that she wouldn't dash off and lead the ghost away? I needed that ghost to follow me. We needed to take our best shot to get rid of it, not for any of us to escape it and meet it another day.

YeeeEEEEEEEooooooooooooooooEEEEEEEEEooooooooooEEEEEEEE EEEE!

I turned the sound back on, and the projector blared at full volume, the crazy music of the Cops matching their antics our makeshift movie screen, dashing about and falling over one another. I just remembered to pick up the meat-stained gloves that Mary had left with me, and I ran as quickly as I could to the east to the intersection that would lead north into the woods.

We hoped that the moving picture would distract the Chookalo long enough that I could get some distance. When I reached the intersection, I stopped and dropped the first glove there. I hid around the corner of the building on the northwest side of the intersection and peeked back at the town square.

Where I had been standing seconds before, the Chookalo, using both claws, tore the movie projector and film into metal and celluloid shreds. The sounds of the musical score screeched and then whirred to a stop.

I don't know if the meat Mary left would have done the trick alone or if Hugh's rabbit made a necessary addition, but the creature had gone into a frenzy even beyond what I had seen it capable of before.

The Chookalo let out a wild howl and then another: the first proclaimed victory over its mechanical foe; the second shrieked its anger that the swipes of its claws drew no living blood, only inanimate matter.

It began looking around—and sniffing.

To me it looked taller than it had, and the claws looked longer. The rolling of those baleful eyes looked more fixated and ruthless.

That could have come from my fear or from the fact that this prey had twice eluded its pursuer, who wasn't accustomed to failing in its hunts.

eeeeeeeeeeeeeeEEEEEEEoheeeeeeeEEEEEoheeeeeeeeeeoh Ah!

It got the scent of the glove I had carried and began to lope east in the direction where I had run.

I sprinted north for the woods, as fast as I could go. I don't believe I have ever run faster, even in the strength and limberness of youth. Terror powered my legs, and I ran so that I felt as though my feet barely hit the ground. A short block from the woods I dropped the second glove.

I couldn't afford to lose speed by looking back. But I could hear. Fear, while it had stripped my other senses of fine detail, left to me the full strength of my hearing.

yeeeeeeeeeeeEEEEEEEEEOOOOOOOOOOOOOOOOOOOOOO
OOOOOOW!

I knew that it had got the scent of the second glove.

The mad wail continued, and it was getting louder as the creature began to catch up to me. I imagined that it was on my heels, and I cursed my imagination.

The sound resolved into a high-pitched shriek—yet it was farther back from me than it had been: the creature had found the second bloody glove.

Normally the Chookalo had seemed to me to move almost silently. I heard then what sounded like feet landing from large leaps.

I hoped the woods could save me and that I could reach the rendezvous in time. The path was barely visible in the moonlight, as shreds of light glimmered down through the foliage, but winding, so that the heavy trees would restrict anything of earthly substance from following a straight course through the woods. The Chookalo, if it were more than a substanceless ghost, as it must be to tear both flesh and metal to ribbons, would have to take the path I took, unless it knew a better one than Ezekiel or unless it chose not to follow me, but to take a path of its own.

I trusted in the ferocity of its vengeance, that it wouldn't on that night give up on its human prey.

I had earlier left my traces of tar to mark my path, but fear and speed took from me the ability to see or sniff them. I ran for my life, turning and dodging my way down the sinuous path as best I could follow it.

I thought I felt hot breath and a lick of fire on the back of my neck.

I hadn't tried to run that far and that fast in years. Suddenly I realized that my lungs were burning from lack of breath—I had no more reserve and must faint from exhaustion in seconds.

The path opened up into a clearing just as I thought I hadn't the strength for one more step. I leaped forward and slid on my belly: right into the first hole that the others had dug.

I had reached the rendezvous, and Polly and Dan were waiting there prepared, if people waiting for a fiery demon can ever call themselves prepared.

My lungs ached, and I had no breath left. I fumbled and found what they had left for me in the center of the hole.

It wasn't a very deep hole—not more than two feet down and maybe ten feet long. The ground was soft and muddy. Trying to suck in air before I fainted, I found a smoke pot and a metal lighter, and I lit the contents of the pot and swung my body away to the south wall of the hole. The pot went up in flames.

Somewhere between consciousness and unconsciousness, I found my memory thrown back to the trenches in France and Belgium.

Bullets overhead in uneven percussion, like some kind of mean-spirited modernist music that the composer intended to unsettle his audience and send them diving under their chairs. The irregular rhythm—pok, pik-pok, pik-pik-pik, pok, rat-tat-tat-tat-tat brrrrrrrrrrrrr, pok, pok, pik, brrrrrrrrrrrr—could, beyond the bursts of earth and flame, drive a person mad. It had no predictability, coming from maybe a hundred different guns of different sorts and ranges. Then the screaming and impossibly loud burst of a shell. Then the sounds of men charging, of men screaming in pain or fear or with the heat of fighting on them. All different, wicked sounds. Darkness: what seemed like days and days of darkness and filth, then a little light, just a little, like a temptation, a hint that to believe the whole thing would someday end was somehow all right, that to believe one could get out alive was sensible and not madness. Then somehow the firing would stop. Whistles would blow, and someone, someone you'd never seen, someone full of youth and joy would bring food, and every tenth time the food was warm and the water clean. You would talk to someone, someone you had never met before, someone from California or Kentucky or Maine or Alberta, someone from New York or Toronto or Chicago or Quebec or from some little town you had never heard of, that no one beyond the few dozen human beings who lived there had ever heard of, and they could do odd and wonderful things: someone could make toys out of scraps of wood and cloth to send home to a niece and nephew, someone could jump onto a table five feet high without running up first, someone could shoot a tin can off a fence post at a hundred yards, someone could sing opera like Caruso, someone could do two hundred, yes two hundred push-ups, someone could take a comb and a handkerchief and play songs with them that would make everyone laugh, someone remembered every joke he had ever heard and could even make up new ones on the spot. Some men could recite whole books of the Bible from memory—amazing and wonderful to listen to them as they spoke, since they spoke with music and belief and not just from memory. And the *whuup!* sound with its puff of dust and blood and uniform that kicks up when one gets shot and sometimes pain, horrible pain, and sometimes just surprise, disbelief that this time it is really you who have been shot, and sometimes death, and sometimes misery and then death, and sometimes the mad laughter that replaces horror and the calling of help! and the praying or cursing wondering about what will happen or simply the, no matter how well one has prepared, DISBELIEF—this can't be happening this can't be happening this can't be happening not to me not to my friend not to my brother, what about mother and father at home what about wife at home what about sweetheart at home and the ghosts, all the ghosts, and what about children children children all the children at home and here in France and Belgium and Germany what will happen to them and how did we who were not so long ago children let this come to pass? how did we do it why did we do it, God, why did we do it? Why, God, do we keep doing it, this war war war the trench, the trench! Protection, no protection, a tomb! it is wet, soaked, flooded, soft, running like a wound with rats and lice and disease I can't get out, it is consuming me, consuming, swimming, not—the mud, it is too thick it will drown us all, grasping, here! Take my hand, get out, get out! Help! pull me, pull, no one else there, pull myself up, now or never, pull myself up and out!

A shriek woke me. I still had little air, but I had consciousness, and I tried to get enough air into my lungs to move. I had to bring myself back from the war and into the present. I had more yet to do on that night in the woods in this human meeting, face to face, with Wiskalo Chookalo.

I didn't see everything that happened. Polly and Dan told me much of it. As far as I can tell here's what happened, from my memory and others'.

Polly and Dan had heard me running through the woods, so they knew the plan had worked that far. They had sent Ezekiel on north over the stream and though the woods beyond to the home of an old friend of his whose house fell nearest to place where the woods broke up. A glen led to a hamlet along another stream beyond the haunts of Uppsala's ghost. Dan and Polly had heard the shouts and wails of the ghost as it pursued its prey through Uppsala and into its own woods. They prepared themselves in their own ways, and they stood ready as I rounded out of the woods and into the clearing.

They saw Wiskalo Chookalo only a few leaps behind me as I slid into the first hole and lit the smoke pot.

Polly had counted on the creature's having some memory, on its being more than a demonic hunting machine. It would remember, she hoped, how the McBride brothers had tried to catch it in a pit of fire, and in the full heat of its anger, it would react immediately to a known obstacle and not stop to think its way around. It was a creature of wrath and vengeance and ferocity, not of reason.

The beast, slowing at the clearing, saw the flame burst from the hole where I hid, and it must have imagined that it once again faced an old strategy.

It perceived a flaming hole in the ground, one that had already consumed the prey it had chased, and beyond that hole stood two human creatures, grim and calm in their courage, who had set the same old trap for it.

It shrieked with joy that it recognized the plot, and it leaped over the hole. Its leap would place it within range to claw the plotters into ribbons and devour them flesh, blood, and bone.

I saw the creature fly over the hole where I sat, and my mind slipped back to an unlikely thought from what I'd read in Dan's study: I remember the passage from *Volsungasaga* about how Sigurd dug the pit to catch the man-dragon Fafnir.

Sigurd had killed the monster by stabbing its soft belly with his sword. I used no sword, and my feckless little fire could do no more harm to the Chookalo than a breath of wind, but it had done its job anyway. I couldn't stop the laugh that comes from small victories.

Even as the creature leaped, it noticed that something about the two creatures on the other side was different than what it knew. They weren't like the others, like the targets of its vengeance with their pale whiteness and their selfish fear and with the smell of murderous blood and killing fire upon them. They were different than the prey.

They were the Others: the human creatures it did not stalk. Those whose blood had been shed by the white strangers, not the strangers who had shed blood so willingly, so joyfully, so monstrously: they stood there now as prey, plotters, equal enemies, the same as those it had ruthlessly pursued, worthy now too of vengeance and pain, like the old ones, the hunted.

Such thoughts as an *atyanlusla* might have, the creature must have had, and they confused it in its wild leap upon its newly discovered enemies, and those thoughts betrayed it. The leap had not quite enough power, and the hunter fell just short of its new prey.

With all the strength and speed that Polly, Dan, and Ezekiel could muster, they had dug a second hole beyond the first. It was deeper and stood nearer the water, so that the ground at its bottom was wet and sticky. The edges were slick and eager to collapse right back into the space from which they had just been dug.

They had covered the hole with a large cloth and had covered the cloth with dirt to make it, in the dark, nearly imperceptible, especially to something running towards it that believed it had just escaped the one dangerous obstacle that stood in its way.

The creature, when it fell, dropped not in the full flight of vengeance on its victims, but into the second pit they had dug. That pit held not fire, but wet, yielding, gripping, muddy earth.

Not very deep, it still held the creature: an earth spirit held in its own element.

From the creature's eyes a bolt of fire flew up into the sky, and a deafening screech echoed through the woods.

The claws immediately flew up over the edge of the pit to pull itself out, but they caught only wet earth and slid back in.

I felt sick for lack of air, but pulled myself out of my own hole and took my post to the south end of the Chookalo's earthy cell.

It stuck in the trench, a trench like that I had once escaped—I felt as if I were back in the war again.

Polly and Dan held no weapons. They had only their courage, their composure, and their prayers, what the uninformed might call magic. They spoke.

The creature growled and snarled, but it didn't wail its horrific scream. It seemed under the spell of their words. For a moment I was, too. The Chookalo glowed bright blue-white, but the earth seemed to absorb its fire: no more flames leaped from its eyes or its body.

I can recognize and speak only a few words and phrases of Oneida. There I could hear two voices, but I could make nothing of what they said. The tones were low, controlled, rhythmic, earthy. Each one spoke, but the speeches didn't coincide. As I learned later, here is what they prayed.

Polly, bathed in blue light, the aura of her own regal spirit, prayed so:

"Mother Earth, take back your own spirit child. Forgive those whose deeds have raised it from the ground. Forgive the violence, the hatred, and the greed. Remember the suffering of their victims, but let the memory be enough, and let the punishment cease. Help us remember that we are your own, and that each day we owe a debt of our survival to you. Help us to remember to care for you even as we care for ourselves. May the Creator find joy in Creation, in the Earth, in humans, in animals, in plants, in the hills and valleys and streams and plains. May we remember that joy and let it fill us, that it may wash away the evils we have done and that we have endured. Mother, take back your spirit child, and let this ground, this tortured earth and the creatures in it, find peace. Let this angry spirit at last find peace and gentle sleep in the earth from which it has come, peace in you, from whom it has come. Creator and Mother Earth, grant us the strength of kindness and the courage that comes from friendship, love, and forgiveness."

And Dan, bathed in white light, prayed so:

"Creator, speak to this Earth our mother. We have lived too long in violence and bloodshed, too long in fear in hatred. Let our ancestors forgive their ancestors, and let us forgive them. I, too, have spilled blood, in lands far away. Bring peace to my spirit that I may speak of peace to this land and its spirits. May I find forgiveness: I acted there not in vengeance, but for love of this place, my place and the place of my people, so that other people in other places might have freedom to love and live in their own lands. I chose an enemy. May the descendants of that enemy forgive me for my bloodshed. May the descendants of those people we defended remember us with respect and honor because we fought for them. May our own people, the Original People and the Newcomers, never again go lightly into battle. May they find peace with one another so that your spirit of vengeance may return to sleep, return to the earth from which our violence brought it. May it find peace, and may we treat our Mother Earth with kindness so that she may never again send the vengeful spirit to remind us that at last we are no more than the animated dust from which it also comes. I ask forgiveness for my own evils and offer forgiveness to all who would take it from me. I pledge this act and every act in your honor, Creator, and in honor of our Mother Earth."

They had the right to pray so: this was their land. My mind raced back to the fields and trenches of the Great War, not so great for those of us who were there. I was with the British Army at Cambria in November 1917 when the Allies unleashed mustard gas against the Germans. The Germans had used it first, they thought, and that gave them the right of retaliation. The wind blew to their advantage, and the commanders believed that they could unleash the terror on their enemies that their enemies had used against them. Yes, I was there.

I had forgotten.

But the result didn't turn out as they planned on that day. The wind shifted and blew the gas, which should have stayed way ahead of the advancing Allied forces, right back onto them, and back toward me as well. We all heard the alarm for gas and had put our masks on immediately.

Yes, I had forgotten that day! I always told myself I had never seen action in a gas attack. But I had: once I had. It was a horrible thing for an army to do, and it was a grave error, tactically and morally, an act of hatred and vengeance.

On that day they poisoned their own troops, their own men.

161

I wasn't in the front line. I was in the rear guard.

All the soldiers had gas masks, but not everyone had thought to use them. As I advanced, a whiff of something, or just intuition, perhaps— *something*—had told me to put on my mask. As the wind changed, the soldiers began retreating. Most had their masks on, though even that wouldn't protect against the burning of exposed skin. Some fumbled, having trouble getting the masks on, and a few had lost or forgotten their masks entirely—men can be foolhardy, even in war. Our officers had told us strictly, long before: in a gas attack, keep your mask on. If you feel pity for a fellow soldier who has been exposed to the gas, do what you can for him, but don't give him your mask. Then the two of you will suffer. The two of you will die. And then neither of you can help the other or anyone else or continue on against the enemy. Use caution and good sense. One death is bad; two deaths are worse.

Neither side was shooting then. Most men stayed forward as their officers had ordered them, but some few came running back, stumbling. Clouds rolled over the field ahead, but I was still safe where I stood, advancing no farther.

Then I saw the cloud, rolling back even to where I stood.

But then I saw a man running toward me. He was a Canadian, a comrade: I could tell from his uniform insignia. "Help!" He made a sound between a shriek and a cough. His face was burned and swollen, and a yellow froth was bubbling from his mouth. "Help! Mask! My mask! Yours!" He tried to cry out, but he could manage only a muffled whisper. He tried to rip the mask from my face to ease his pain, not thinking that he might cause me the same suffering as his own. In such an instance few humans can call up compassion: survival and the drive to stanch pain take over, and instinct drives a person hard and violently. He clawed wildly at my face, scratching my neck, trying to get off my mask. I would not let him take it.

And then he fell slack.

With great effort I picked him up and threw him over my shoulder— not an easy thing to lift a limp body—and began running back toward our rear-guard.

I found a medic in probably not much more than a minute.

The wind had switched again, and any gas left in the air was blowing back away from us again, taking its suffering and death to other men with other allegiances. The medic was not even wearing a mask any longer.

"What's wrong—" he started to say, and then, "Oh: put him down here. Stretcher! You, back there, bring that stretcher here right now! Hurry! You, soldier!" he said to me, "get back up there! Your unit will need you in the front lines. Show some courage!"

I was too shocked even to nod. I just turned and ran back the way I had come, back into the battle. I took a few shots that day, but I don't think I could have hit anything standing right in front of me. I was shaken, almost too shaken to stand. I couldn't resolve for myself having kept that mask. I had followed an order, but had I done right, or had I committed an unpardonable crime?

That night, as the battle continued, draped in darkness split by shooting stars of gunfire, I saw something. I remember seeing or imagining something strange and terrifying: a large figure rising up out of the ground, something glowing green-white and wailing like hurricane-winds, moving on strong and sinewy legs and swinging its deadly claws at anyone, Allied or German, who dared or had the misfortune to cross its path. Had I seen it—the ghost, the *Chookalo*—before, or had I seen something like it? Or had fear and weariness conflated memory and presence in the moment of final confrontation with a living monster?

The Chookalo had turned away from Polly and Dan and fixed its eyes on me. It looked as if it were swimming, treading water, rather than fumbling in wet earth. It swung its baleful eyes on me, threw its claws over the edge of the pit toward me, tried to latch onto firm ground. I looked back at it, but directed my gaze away from its eyes. What Polly and Dan were doing, I must do, too.

I don't have the innate, creative spirituality that Dan and Polly have. I could find no words to make a prayer of my own. But my mind slipped back to the prayer that Hugh and I had spoken earlier, that I had tried to remember so that I might do my part, so that I too might glow as Polly's dream saw me glow. I felt not like a red glow, but like a shadow. I had tried to remember that prayer, but in the heat of the moment I couldn't bring it back, couldn't grasp it.

The creature's growling was intensifying again, and it was beginning to succeed in drawing itself out of the earth and toward me. Clearly our plan needed all three of us to succeed.

My eyes wouldn't focus, and I glanced past the Chookalo. Straight beyond it, between Polly and Dan, I saw another spirit, a ghost, bright white, with black spots, in the shape of a large dog. The sight of it helped calm my thoughts.

I tried again to remember the words of the prayer, which floated into my thoughts and then away again. And then I found them, bobbing up into my thoughts like a buoy. I repeated as well as I could, as I had practiced earlier, the Franciscan prayer of my childhood:

Lord, make me an instrument of peace.

Where I find hatred, let me share kindness.

Where I find injury, help me heal pain.

Where I find discord, let me bring quiet.

Where people need faith, let me find faith.

Where I make errors, let me find truth.

Where I feel despair, let me bring hope.

In the darkness, may I find light.

Where there is sorrow, may I speak consolation.

That was as nearly as I could remember it at the time: I know I didn't get it quite right. Even my early practice hadn't got me that far. But I don't think that mattered. Even as I spoke, the growling and scratching of the creature calmed. The feeling meant more than the words, and as I spoke the prayer, I grew calmer. Breath had come back to me. I breathed deeply between lines of prayer, and in the very presence of the ghost a wave of calm swept through and over me as I spoke aloud to God.

I realized that I had never hated the Chookalo. I had feared it. I had wanted to destroy it, to relieve that place of it, but I didn't want to give it pain. I wanted it to return to the elements that had borne it so that it might never trouble humans again. Those thoughts comforted me.

But that was a silly thing to hope. Only the innocent think the earth benign to its creatures. "Nature never did betray the heart that loved her": Wordsworth, yes, the line came from Wordsworth, and only a true Romantic would speak it or believe it. The human being who has seen exploding shells and poisoned gas knows that we humans tear the world apart in our greed and wrath, but even if we didn't, anyone who has known earthquake, flood, wildfire, monsoon, bitter, icy cold, drought, hurricane or tornado knows that the earth can and will shake us off whether we love her or not. We must love her for the time she gives us and give her no reason to shake us off sooner than she otherwise will.

The thought struck me that what before had been the blue-white glow of the creature had dimmed. It had become a pale white, and it was now turning to a sickly yellow-green: it reminded me of the killing fields, the jaundice of bodies losing blood or turning gangrenous, of the air poisoned with gas and the smoke of exploding shells, the dull yellow of a field fallowed by bombs and war implements and the tread of thousands of men, tearing up and out the grass and the flowers and the trees that should have graced that once brilliantly decorated garden that had become a stretched-out grave for anything that dared cross over it.

I tried to choke down the distraction and continue my prayer. I could just see on the limits of my perception two glowing embers: Polly to my left, Dan to my right, as they continued their prayers. They had drawn the spirit back into its earth, and I had to do best to try to keep it there. They had subdued it, and I had to pray with all my heart to keep it from rising again.

I couldn't help myself from allowing my eyes to meet the Chookalo's eyes once more, whatever the danger.

How different now—when I had first seen those eyes, they had spat fire and hatred and hunger and vengeance. Now they looked tired and quieted, unfocused. They glowed not fire-white, but a dull green, the way grass looks just at dawn, before the bright sun turns it emerald. They did not shout wrath and threat. They hinted age and sleep. Without my thinking about it, my prayer changed to something more personal, something kinder even than Francis' prayer, if that's possible, and I prayed in my own voice:

"Find rest now, perturbed spirit. Let the earth take you back. Find sleep in your own place, your own element. May we do nothing to disturb your rest. It's all right: you can let go of us now. Drop gently into the lap of our Mother. Your time here is done. No more anger: peace, spirit, peace."

I think that's what I said. That or something like it. An odd thing to say to a being that had murdered, that had torn its victims limb from limb. But it wasn't a spirit of reason. It was a spirit of vengeance. It had got vengeance, and it was passing into an oblivion of sleep. For good, I hoped—for good.

The eyes, with the last of their pale green glow, looked into mine with something like understanding and resignation. The face turned away, toward Dan and then toward Polly. The body was sinking further into the earth. The legs had disappeared under the ground, and now the torso was sinking, too. It uttered sounds, no longer the mad screech that froze its hearers in utter terror, but something more like cold sighs, a lament—the sounds of self-elegy. The wet ground seemed to whirl beneath the ghostly body whose spark was slowing dying as the bulbous head floated on the mud.

We stood there for some time. The lights around Polly and Dan faded, as did the third light opposite, the canine spirit that had joined our ritual. The first rays of false-dawn sprang gently over the eastern horizon, and the clearing in the woods opened up with first light.

The large head drifted downward as though into a whirlpool. The ears floated for a few seconds on the viscous ground. The eyes turned up to the sky and seemed to drink in the light, something they may never have seen so fully before. And then they closed and disappeared into the earth.

The last of Wiskalo Chookalo had sunk again into its own element.

The three of us, Polly, Dan, and I, eased our way over to the edge of the pit.

The canine spirit looked upward and disappeared in the risen sun's first light.

The hole wasn't even very big or very deep. But it had sufficed. The bottom of it, which looked watery before, was already drying. The ground shone with a hint of something midway between dew and frost.

"Pretty morning," Dan said. "But it's going to turn cold soon."

"Yes," Polly replied. "It's that time of year."

"You ready to go home?" Dan asked.

"Yes," Polly said. "I'm feeling a little shaky. Must be hungry."

"Will we see you again before you go, Hank?" Dan asked.

"Yes," I said, "if you don't mind. I promised to be out of town one way or another this morning. Looks like I can at least leave under my own power. But I'll stop at your place first before I leave. I have that Smith & Wesson to return to Michael Smith."

"Say good-bye to Mary and Clayton for us, Hank Peck," Polly said.

"I'll walk that way with you!" a voice called out from the woods across the stream to north. It was Ezekiel.

"Couldn't get myself to leave you folks all alone," he said. "Not that I'd have knowed what to do. You three put on quite a show, and looks like you took good care of old Chookalo."

"Good to see you, Ezekiel," I said. "Polly Cooper, do you think we did take care of that spirit—for good?"

"I'd be afraid to say *for good.* The *ohsúhtok* has gone back where it should go, into the earth, and I think for now its powers have ended, at least here on this plot of earth. I don't say that it won't come back here or elsewhere if people deserve it."

"Then I hope we'll do our best not to deserve it," Ezekiel said.

"Amen," I added.

We walked down the path for a bit without speaking. Polly and Don walked on east and south, following a second path, and Ezekiel and I went straight south to town. I felt lost in some memories that hadn't come to mind in many years—not good memories, but I could at last make sense of them. I felt oddly calm, considering what all of us had seen in the very short time I had been in and around Uppsala. You might expect that after what we'd seen, something most people would call *supernatural,* that the hair would still be standing straight up on each of our heads. Yet as I walked my thoughts through the steps of that experience, especially with the ghost, it seemed to me not at all supernatural, but as natural as anything else you might see. The unnatural acts had already occurred: the bullyings, the thievings, the killing of human beings by other human beings. It seemed natural as day to me that the earth herself should rise up against us, to take action against the evils we have committed.

Finally Ezekiel broke our silence. "That was really something, what you three did out there. I tried to do what Polly had said, to follow the path and keep walking north beyond the woods to a safe place. But I just couldn't do it. I don't know what I could have done to help. Had no idea at all! But I couldn't just leave you there, either! What was that you did: praying? That's all it was? No magic, no spells, just common, everyday prayer? Now that's something. Really something. You'd think someone would have thought of that years ago. But old Chookalo's quiet in that earth, I'll bet, and if folks get to doing things they shouldn't again, it'll come back—that's my guess."

"Do you believe people can change, Mr. Grimsson?"

"Do I? Well, they have to want to. You can only change something if you want to. Habits run deep. Try to get a man to stop drinking or smoking or cheating on his wife: he can do it *if he wants to*. Problem is, most people don't want to."

"Yes, that is the problem."

I thought I heard a dog barking somewhere ahead.

"You know the Book of Ezekiel, my namesake?"

"I think I remember some of it."

"It foretells the fall of Jerusalem and the destruction of the great temple because of the sins of the people."

"Reminds you of Uppsala? If I remember, the book also foretells the founding of a new and better city, a new home for the people. Things don't go easily, but they get better, especially when the people try to do better."

"You're a learned man, Hank."

"I've seen a little of the world, Mr. Grimsson. I have much more to learn."

We had passed out of the woods, and the back fence of Clayton Schmidt's house came into view.

We had one more adventure ahead that day—it was after all barely morning, and we were still in Uppsala, Wisconsin.

There we saw Florin Huggins with his pants caught on the gate that led through the fence into Clayton's yard. Cassie the dog stood in front of him and barked at him every time he tried to move.

Clayton and Mary looked like they had got there just before we had, and they were wondering what to do with Florin. His face was red, and he was cursing at the dog, who didn't let that trouble her at all.

Mary looked at Ezekiel and me in astonishment and ran right up: she tried to throw a huge hug around both of us at once.

"Mary and I are much happier to see you than our friend Florin here. Our faithful dog has caught us a thief, I think!" Clayton said.

"I'm no thief!" Florin yelled, and he spat at the dog. Cassie jumped and took a nip at him, and he cowered against the fence.

"Maybe not: probably a would-be killer instead. I found him here just a couple minutes ago. I stayed with Mary last night, and when I came over this morning, I found that the observation room had been broken into. Lucky for me Cassie was guarding it, and she wasn't going to let in anyone, not even the Chookalo."

"Let me out of here!" Florin yelled.

"Hold still, Florin, and I'll try to get you lose. You've just got your pants stuck on the door latch." Florin was wearing a kind of overall, and the fancy latch had caught and twisted one of his belt loops and a shoulder strap.

Clayton gave a tug and pulled Florin loose, but in the process the shoulder strap tore.

"Look what you done!" Florin said and took a poke at Clayton, almost knocking him down.

"See what I mean, Mr. Grimsson? People don't change so easily."

I made sure that Florin had missed, and I steadied Clayton. Meantime, Florin Huggins slipped behind me. I knew that kind of man and what he'll do. He had a grudge against me, too.

I caught his arm just as he was throwing a sucker punch.

"One more lesson," I said, "and then I'm leaving town, so please learn this one." I twisted his arm so that he fell to one knee, and I grabbed his elbow to hold him down. I saw a knife, still in its sleeve, tied under the shirt of his overalls. A threw a quick left hook and stopped it just short of his temple: I took care that he could see it. Then I pulled the knife from his sleeve and tossed it over the fence.

"Don't do that ever again to anyone. Remember that I could have killed you, and I let you go. Remember that you should have apologized to Mr. Schmidt, and you didn't. Think about those things, and become a better man."

I released his elbow, pulled him up by the shoulder, and gave him a push toward town. He took a couple shuffle steps to catch his balance, rubbed his shoulder, and continued walking toward town without turning back toward us. I hoped he had learned that lesson, but I feared he had not. Most of us need a long time and many lessons to understand mercy and kindness, whether it comes from God or other human beings—or even from animals. Cassie could have hurt him, too, if she'd wished. She, too, had been merciful.

"My brothers ain't gonna like this when they hear about it," Florin spat out as he hurried off.

Cassie jumped right up into my arms and began licking my face. She looked like she needed breakfast.

"Anything stolen?" I asked. "Or do we just have more glass to fix?"

"I don't think he took anything. He probably wanted to hurt someone, though. I found a club with a metal plug that he must have used to shatter the glass. He either dropped it or Cassie knocked it out of his hands—he must not have been prepared to face our watchdog!"

"He had that knife, too," I said. "I don't think he's ready to let things go yet."

"What happened last night? We heard an awful noise here in town and then in the woods. Did Polly Cooper's plan work? Is Wiskalo Chookalo gone?"

"Yes," I said, "I think it's gone. For now, at least."

"You shoulda seen what I saw," Ezekiel said. "It was something. Really something. They didn't even fight with it. Fighting it would never have worked anyway. I always knowed that, and I'm glad you didn't try. Ol'

Chookalo's gone, and the place feels different already. Just breathe that air! It even smells different. I'm glad I lived to see this day."

"I wonder, though, if things have changed enough so that the people will change. That's the main thing. Otherwise, I believe the spirit will come back. If not now, someday," I said.

"I think Hank's right," Mary said. "But what can we do? Can we even convince the people of what happened? How will they know?"

"For one thing, I'll tell them," Ezekiel said. "Here's my idea: we go to the town square. We call everyone to come. We tell them the whole story. And they'll feel the difference for themselves, like a sickness has ended. How can they not feel that?"

"Some of them will come armed, I'll bet," Clayton said. "And Hank, you must be exhausted! How can you face another battle without getting some sleep?"

"Exhausted, yes, but I don't think I can sleep yet. Let's get this job good and done. You take the gun, Clayton, to protect you and Mary. I'm going to face them unarmed."

"I'm not sure that's smart, Hank" Clayton said.

"I'm not sure either. But it feels right. By rights I could be dead three times over. The spirit didn't get me. Maybe I can survive one more confrontation in Uppsala, Wisconsin, and I hope this one won't have to be a battle."

"That was just a demon," Mary said. "You'll be facing people now, Hank, and they can be far meaner."

The three of us had some coffee, and Cassie got a little breakfast, and then the four of us sauntered out to the town square.

The square looked a mess: Wiskalo Chookalo had torn the moving picture equipment to bits and had slashed down most of the gazebo. A number of the townsfolk were already out looking around. A boy had found the dead rabbit that Hugh had set out as bait for the creature: it was lying right in the center of dais in the middle of the square, still dead but whole. The creature had placed it there carefully.

"There's the man responsible!" a woman shouted out, pointing at me.

"What do you say we start cleaning up?" Clayton asked.

"Listen here, you people!" Ezekiel called out. "I'm going to have more to say in just a bit. But Letty, this man is no more responsible for the Chookalo than the Indians were, and I've heard you say that enough times. You should walk right up here and shake this man's hand. He and his friends—and they're our friends, too, you'd better know—have driven off that ghost! It's gone, and we're free of it, as long as you folks don't decide to be stupid and bring it back again."

A rumble of voices rose up in response to Ezekiel's brief speech: Impossible! Can it be? I don't believe it! A miracle! Could they really do that! It's a hoax!

Ezekiel continued, "Now some of you folks, you just get your neighbors out here. We're going to use this town square for what it's supposed to do. We're going to have our first town meeting in a generation, and everyone in Uppsala is going to know what happened here last night and what can happen now any night we want. The night is ours again! The ghost is gone! Hurry up, now: get everyone here quickly as you can!"

Some of the people stayed, but some, especially the younger ones, ran off and started whooping it up along the streets and avenues. Within a few minutes more people showed up around the square, and gradually more and more filtered in.

Then what I thought had to happen did in fact happen.

Three men pushed through the crowd: one had a large club with a metal end, one had a whip, and the third had a handgun. Behind them came two others with handguns. The Huggins brothers I knew, and the others looked, as well as I could tell, like two of the men who had accosted me in the alley behind the diner.

"Now you men, put down those weapons!" Ezekiel called out. "You should be thanking this man. He's freed this town of a plague. He's got rid of the Chookalo! You should be shaking his hand and giving him the key to the city, if we had such a thing."

"I don't believe none of that," Galen said, "but I know what he has done, and he's gonna pay for it."

"The Chookalo will come back tonight, and it will do even worse than it's ever done, and it's his fault!" Ivan yelled.

"He's made it personal now," Florin said, swinging his club, "and

I'm gonna kill him for it, and then I'm gonna break you up, Clayton Schmidt. Now you just put down that gun you got, or I'll shoot you first." He had a gun in a holster at his waist.

I stepped out in front to meet them.

"Just so everyone knows. Wiskalo Chookalo is gone. It disappeared this morning right back into the earth. If the people of this town can keep peace with one another and with strangers, I believe you'll never see it again. If you insist on fighting and killing, I suspect it will come back. You have it in your power to make things better. But if you can't make this choice, kill me now, and leave the others alone, and let that be the end of it."

"I heard enough of you," Ivan said, whirling his whip above his head. "We're going to kill you, all right, and after that we'll do just as we please."

"Then you'll have to kill me, too," Clayton said, stepping up beside me to my right.

"Fine by me," Florin said, aiming his gun at Clayton.

"And me, too," Mary said, stepping up to my left.

"Ain't gonna kill no woman, Mary," Galen said, "but if you insist on a beating, you'll get it," and he stepped forward with his club.

"You men go home and leave these folks alone. I saw them stop the Chookalo with my own eyes!" Ezekiel was doing his best.

"Shut up, crazy old man," Galen said. "Nobody believes you."

"But I saw it, too!" another thin, shaky voice arose, weak, but loud enough to hear. It came from Alma Jones.

"I followed you out last night, Ezekiel, into the woods. I saw which way you went, and I came out, too. I was worried about you, about all of you. I was in the woods. I saw it! Saw the ghost, like it was caught in a whirlpool, sink right down into the earth! And they didn't do it with guns. They did it with prayer, something we could use more of around here."

"Alma!" Ezekiel said. "You did that for me?"

"Shut up, y'old bat!" Florin screeched, and the attackers again stepped forward.

I was trying to resolve myself not to fight, to accept whatever blows rained on me. It wasn't easy, and I'm not sure I could have done it.

173

A number of shots rang out in rapid fire, echoing through the square.

Hugh and Nick McGrath strode out of the crowd, holding Winchesters: they had fired warning shots to get everyone's attention, and they had got it. No one moved.

"That's enough," Hugh said. "Nobody's going to kill anyone here today. We have a promise to keep to Hank Peck, and he's leaving town, for good, right now. Right, Hank?"

"Join us or go home, Hugh," Florin said. "You can't side with this boy! Join us, or we'll kill you, too."

"Had about enough of you, Florin," Hugh said. "Come on, Hank: I'll walk you down to the railroad myself."

Another shot rang out, a single shot: Florin had aimed at Hugh and fired.

But, having an injured right shoulder, he shot with his left hand, and he missed.

I had hurt him just enough, taking him down outside of Clayton's backyard, so that he failed to hit Hugh. That's enough for one man to hurt another man.

In that instant Clayton stepped forward and caught Florin flush on the jaw with a straight punch. Florin went down and dropped his gun. Someone else from the crowd hurriedly kicked it away.

Nick McGrath leveled his gun at Ivan Huggins. "Put the whip down, Ivan, and I mean it," he said. "If anyone has a grudge, I do, and I'm telling you I don't. Hugh has talked some sense into me. Lucas caused his own trouble, just like you're doing now. Hank's not to blame. You two men back there: you know you don't shoot as well as Hugh and I do, so don't touch your guns."

That left Galen Huggins. I stepped in front of Mary and toward Galen.

"The two of us, then," Galen said. "That's fine by me. At least I won't chicken out. I can still beat your brains in."

He stepped forward and swung his club hard and low as if he were going to take the legs out from beneath me, but that was just a feint. He whirled in around and came straight down toward the crown of my head.

174

I dodged, and the metal end of the club rang out against the stone where I had been standing.

The swing unbalanced Galen, and I grabbed the club and wrenched it from his hands. Before he could regain balance, I kicked him in the leg and knocked him over, and then I stepped back a pace.

"Get up," I said.

He did, stumbling.

I tossed the club back to him.

"Swing it again," I said. "This time I won't dodge. Swing it with all your strength and get the vengeance you want. You may just succeed in bringing the Chookalo back, if you'd like. That's not up to me. But what you do now is up to you."

Galen Huggins let out a growling shriek, and he raised the club above his head to strike.

But he didn't bring it down on my head.

By then the people in the crowd were against him.

He looked at the faces of all of the Uppsalans standing around. They looked back at him with unmitigated disgust.

"Don't do it, Galen," Ezekiel said gently. "Be a better man than that."

Galen shouted another anguished cry, and he dropped the club, turned around and ran away, disappearing out through the back of the crowd.

I thought of something. "Ezekiel, does Uppsala have a mayor?"

"Mayor? No. Haven't had that for years and years. Haven't had any town offices."

"The people could do worse than to make you their mayor," I said.

"What about you, Hank Peck?" Ezekiel asked. "What don't you stay on here? You can be our mayor. You're the one who done all the work, you and the two Oneidas. They can be your town council. Them and maybe Hugh McGrath, who is turning out to be a pretty solid citizen at last."

"I can't stay," I said.

"Why not?" Mary asked. "I agree with Ezekiel. We haven't had a man like you around here before. You could help us change."

"Ezekiel's your man," I said. "He's brave, and he knows this place

175

better than anyone, and he's lived here long enough to love it, despite all that's gone on here." I looked at Hugh. "And I made a promise."

"That's a promise I wouldn't mind seeing you break," Hugh said. "It's a promise I got out of you before I knew better."

"I made a promise to you and to the town to leave today. What kind of man would I be if I broke it, especially for my own benefit? And I made another promise I have yet to keep. I promised my aunt in Duluth that I'd get there to see her. I'd like to keep that promise before winter settles in and travel gets too hard."

"It's probably already snowing in Duluth," Alma Jones said. "I have a cousin up there."

"I'll say 'hello' for you."

Clayton came up to me and took my hand and shook it firmly. "Never thought I'd hit another man," he said.

"Did you like doing it?" I asked.

"No!"

"Good. That means you won't do it again unless you absolutely must."

"Hank, there's nothing we can say or do for you that would be enough," Mary said. "But can't we do something?"

"Yes," I said. "You can offer me a little breakfast and then see me off."

HOOOooooooot, HOOT! HOOT!

"Early train today," Ezekiel said. "You can take the later one."

A Good Story is Worth Telling

"So you went on to Duluth?" I asked. Hank had finished his story, and he drained the last of his cold coffee.

"I did," Hank answered. "Nothing else to do but that. The Uppsalans, at least the better among them, gave me a proper hero's send-off. But they needed to bring their town back to life, and they needed to do it themselves. I asked one thing of them: that they make a proper thanks to Polly Cooper and Dan Cornelius. They were the real heroes."

"Do you know if they did that?"

"I didn't take the later train on that day. Before I left, I walked south of town and spent two days with Dan and Polly. I visited the Oneida hamlet in the south woods and returned the gun I'd borrow to Michael Smith there. The morning when I did leave, several of the people from Uppsala came to their door and invited Polly and Dan and Michael to a gathering, a big party, celebrating the town's freedom from its ghost. I'd already gone when they got there, but the party wasn't for me anyway. They wanted, rightly, to show appreciation to Polly and Dan. It was subdued, even quiet—but it lasted well into the evening, well after dark. No one had any problems, either during the party or getting home afterward.

"I got a letter from Dan at my aunt's house in Duluth a couple weeks later telling me about that gathering and saying that a number of the Oneidas had gone to it. They wouldn't exactly say that they felt welcome, but at least they no longer felt hated, and a number of the Uppsalans were genuinely warm and friendly: Mary and Clayton, Ezekial and Alma, even Hugh McGrath—he knew what his Oneida friends had done for him, and he hadn't even recognized them as friends. As I understand it, the Huggins brothers had already moved to Horton, and the folks in Uppsala never saw them there again."

"Do you stay in touch with anyone there?"

"Well, not in the last couple years, but I did until then. Dan Cornelius died about two years back: he and Clayton were the last two who wrote me. Dan was a good man and lived a good, long life: he was a little older than I am now. I'm hoping that Clayton is still all right, since I haven't heard from him since Dan's death—Clayton's the one who wrote me about that."

"How about the others?"

"As far as I know, Polly Cooper's still alive. She'd be in her eighties now. She married the Doxtators' son, and the two of them became the wise folk of their clan. Had a couple children: one became a physician, and one became a professor, first at Madison but now, if I remember right, at the Oneida's own college.

"Here's something: not only did Ezekiel Grimsson become the first mayor of Uppsala in years and years, but he and Alma Jones got married: he was eighty-two then, and she was, I think, seventy-six? They both lived well into their nineties, almost a hundred. For all the trouble it caused, the ghost did those two no harm, and I'm eternally grateful for that.

"Mary Schmidt, who ran the diner, married Ezekiel's grandson. They kept the diner together for a bit, then moved to southern California to join Clayton. Oh, yes: Clayton wanted to learn more about the moving pictures, so he went out there and got involved in the movie industry. His work in electronics got him into military intelligence for a while during the Second World War. He's the one who gave my daughter her break in movie work when she moved out there after college. Mary had a couple kids and stayed out there. Clayton stayed in touch with many people in Wisconsin, Uppsalans and Oneida, and finally moved back. Who'd believe that, huh? Move from sunny California back to snowy Wisconsin.

"Michael Smith, the Oneida who leant me his pistol, became the first official sheriff of Uppsala, but he stayed at it only a few years. He moved up to northern Wisconsin and took a post of some kind with the tribe up there.

"Hugh McGrath: now there's kind of a sad story. He became mayor of Uppsala when Ezekiel couldn't do it anymore, but that was after the Second Great War. Hugh did two years in the Pacific theater, but got wounded badly there and honorably discharged. He was still a young man in his fifties, so he set out to make Ezekiel's dream come true: that, like in the Bible book, Uppsala would become a new and better place, so that maybe people would start to come in from the outside. That never did happen much, though: young people want to go to the cities, not to the small towns. I think he'd had his eye on Mary Schmidt: she was quite pretty—did I tell you that? But he died early. Hunting accident, so people said: shot to death—I think he wasn't even sixty.

"The next day after Hugh's death some boys found Florin Huggins' body in an almost iced-over pond over by Horton. They'd heard him calling out for help the night before, but no one liked him well enough to go out and look for him. One of the boys found his rifle at the bottom of the pond in the spring. I don't think anyone checked to see if that was the gun used to kill Hugh.

"Oh, and Cassie: we can't forget her. I was going to leave her with Dan and Polly: tough for a dog to travel with a hobo. But she got loose and followed me down to the tracks. She ran right beside me as I was boarding the train, so I picked her up and tossed her in and jumped in right behind her. She was a good traveling companion: even the man we hitched with to Duluth was glad to have her along. She settled in nicely at my aunt's house, and she lived another ten years, though she was no pup when she found me. That was some dog.

"You're wondering, too, about the ghost. I never heard that anyone saw Wiskalo Chookalo in Uppsala or anywhere near ever after. These days the news media are all over. If anyone heard that unearthly wailing in these times, everyone would know about it. In many ways we deserve such hauntings now as much as folks did then. We still kill for no reason, and we're tearing up the earth worse than ever. Can't imagine why the earth spirits don't rise up against us. Maybe we've dug them all up or chased them all out—and we probably think ourselves better off for it. But to my way of thinking, as scary as those spirits were, our earth was better for their presence: better and holier when the land can and will speak for itself. I don't think it does that anymore, though we may just be in the proverbial calm before the storm.

"As for me, I did get to Duluth. Dan was going to get another horse, and the two of us were going to ride north for a few days toward Minnesota. But that seemed to me like I'd be causing him too much trouble, so after a couple days with them—and I've never met more hospitable people in all my life—I slipped out really early one morning and caught that day's first train as easily as you please. Remember that sharp s-curve I told you about just west of Uppsala? Yes, I waited there, and the train slowed down, and I hopped on just as if they were waiting for me: no armed guards. Rode for a few hours, then walked north for a day or two, and finally hitched a ride with a fella all the way to Duluth. He was so proud of his 1930 Cadillac that he said he gave rides to strangers all the time just to show it off. Impressive car: long thing, sixteen cylinders, I think he said, with big, fancy white-walled tires. I think that was the only car I ever actually liked. He was a working man, too, but he'd come up with a better design for tires that had made him a lot of money, so he bought himself that car as a reward.

"My aunt was very glad to see me—several days later than she'd expected me, but at least I kept my promise to get there. I've done pretty well at keeping my promises in this life. She made me feel welcome, and I had family again for the first time in a long time. She remarried—did I tell you her second husband had died?— a good man with a couple older children. His wife had died, too, of pneumonia after a bad winter. I lived with them for a couple years and worked in a steel plant and then a cement plant. I went up north yet from there and worked in the iron mines for a time, and then came back to Duluth. My aunt was doing fine, so, during the Second War, I went back east and worked in a metal foundry to help with the war effort. I could have served in the army again—I was just forty-one when it started—but I couldn't get myself to go over there to kill again. I thought we'd done that job already, but politicians over there got in the way and kicked up hatred again, as they always do. I helped in the way I could: after work I volunteered with the military recruiting and getting young people through their basic training, with some simple self-defense and marksmanship for the new recruits. I wanted nothing more than to see all those people come home safe. I wanted to see us keep this earth a planet worth living on.

"During the war I married an Ohio girl, Mary Lou was her name. We heard about a little dairy farm back here in Wisconsin for sale dirt-cheap: this is it. We bought it and moved back. Sold off the dairy equipment and part of the land years ago and just kept the house and barn. Mary Lou died a year ago, and that's the last and the saddest thing of all that I have to tell you. She was one fine woman: kind, devoted, artistic. She used to make wood sculptures of animals and all sorts of odd and grotesque creatures—no, I never told her about the Chookalo. I feared she'd think I was crazy—or that she'd make a sculpture that looked like it! For an artist she was a very practical person. We had the one daughter: a lovely girl, if I do say so myself. But that's about it: what other people heard about Uppsala, they heard from someone else, not me.

"You must be pretty tired now with listening, young fella, because I'm sure tired of talking. Here, have a beer with me before you go—I drink one occasionally these days to calm myself down when I get riled up. Only one, and not often."

Night had long since fallen, and I didn't know how to begin to tell Hank how grateful I felt to have heard his story. I'd done my best to remember to keep feeding new tapes in the recorder and to keep up with my notes, though often I got so caught up in the story that I just sat and listened—that accounts for any omissions or inconsistencies that you find in the story.

"You've been a good listener," Hank added, "so I'm going to tell you just one more thing. You're not going to believe this, but after I saw Wiskalo Chookalo, after I'd looked in its eyes, I never did quite sleep again. Oh, I'll drop off now and then, but I don't sleep well and long, no more than a few minutes. I can tell by your eyes that you don't believe that. I know the physicians say a person can't live for too long without at least some sleep. But I haven't slept well in almost sixty years. I set myself up a little blacksmith shop in the barn, there. Tried to learn more of the old skills my father had—just for a pastime, not to use them for anything. Folks would sometimes come to me for metal work after I retired. Went up to Door County a few years ago to learn from a young metal smith who still practices the old ways. I normally go out there to the barn at night, summer or winter, and tinker until other folks wake up and get busy with their day. Mary Lou was a sound sleeper, and I believe she thought I was just an early riser. I'd have coffee ready for her every morning when she woke up. Mostly that's just been since we came back here to Wisconsin, the smithing work. Some things we're born to, I suspect—what's that the scientists call it? Genetics, that's right.

"But, you know, I think I will sleep well tonight. In fact, telling my tale to someone seems to have helped me ease my mind. I've never told it to anyone—bits and pieces, but never the whole story. Felt almost like a prayer to tell it. Yes, I think I'll sleep well tonight, if you'll excuse me. You know your way back? It's not too hard to find, even in the dark. Just go right back the way you came. The town has even put up a couple street lamps along that road, and you've got a fine, clear, full moon to light your way. Just like the moon, a little fuller, though, than the night we put old Chookalo to rest.

"And just one more thing I'd ask you. Don't go making out that I'm the hero of this story. The real heroes were Polly Cooper and Daniel Cornelius: they forgave people who didn't deserve forgiving, and they worked out the plan, and they helped me remember how to pray."

"I can't thank you enough, Mr. Peck, for telling me your story." I held out my hand, and he grasped it and shook it: it was a healthy young man's handshake still.

"You're welcome, son. You're welcome. Did me more good than it's done you, I'm sure. I'd offer you a place to stay, but you'll be more comfortable in town. I think I'll be sleeping for a long time. You should stop and see Clare at the diner for breakfast in the morning: she's a nice young woman. Still single, I think."

He tipped his hat, and I think he winked, and he drew himself inside his house with a heavy but contented sigh.

I collected my gear and—he was right—made it back into town with no trouble and stayed the night there in a small motel.

Next morning I got up late and went to the diner. Clare was there again, and she got a nice breakfast for me. She asked if I'd had a good talk with Hank Peck. I told her I'd never had such a good talk or heard such a story before.

"What did he tell you about?" Clare asked.

'He told me a ghost story."

"Do you believe him?"

That one was harder to answer.

"Mr. Peck told me about something that happened in the '30s, southwest of here, I think, in a town called Uppsala. Have you ever heard of it?"

"Uppsala? No. Is it near here? He's not from here originally. I think I heard he came from Ohio. He and his wife are the sweetest people—though he's by himself now since she died, not too long ago. I have one of her sculptures here that I can show you—it's really good. He used to have some strange looking people visit him—they'd have lunch here sometimes—though not many go out there anymore that I've seen or heard of. I take him food from the diner that he orders, and I get groceries for him sometimes—he always gives me a nice tip. He always loves the root soup—I make it myself. A real old-time gentleman—I don't think he could ever hurt a fly."

"Do you mind if I stay in touch for a bit?"

"With him or with me?"

"Both, if that's all right. I may have more questions."

"Sure."

"I need to go through my notes once I get home. I got a lot from just one evening of Mr. Peck's storytelling."

"Are you going to write a book about him?"

"Maybe. I think so. Yes."

"Wow. Have you written any books before?"

"Yes, a couple. Nothing important, though."

"Be sure to let me know if you write Mr. Peck's story: I'd love to read it. I'll bet a lot of people around here would. What did you say that town name was? Uppsala? I'll write it down and ask around to see if anyone's heard of it. We have a few people who come in here who are interested in local history or Wisconsin history. Someone's got to know about it."

I finished the breakfast Clare had made me, wished her well, and drove home.

The next day I had classes, so I couldn't get back right away to my notes on Hank Peck's story. It would have seemed like the folklore I usually study if it hadn't all been so vivid. And the way he told it: the story seemed like fantasy or horror, but the delivery made it seem to me like history—right from the person who had lived it. Who am I to say it wasn't true? By Monday night, after the first day of classes, I was itching to get back to it, to go through it again and get it all down clearly and succinctly. I wanted more details, and I wanted to know more about the man's life, but I didn't want to be bothering him with a phone call every day. I would have loved to talk with his doctor about his sleep issues, but that was neither possible nor ethical.

Clare called me the following Saturday: she had checked on Uppsala, and a couple of the older residents said they had heard of it, but they thought the name had been changed—they didn't know who had done that or when, and they didn't know the new name.

I called the University library and asked a research librarian there to look it up for me. She needed a week of going through old maps before she could call back, but she'd finally found Uppsala on one old map, from the '20s.

"I don't think it was ever a very big town," she said, "maybe five hundred people or a little more? So most maps wouldn't have it anyway. The more recent ones that try to list every little town in the state still don't have it at all. I'm guessing your friend is right that they've changed the name."

I thanked her for her help—she had really gone to a lot of trouble—and the fact that the town had appeared on at least one map encouraged me. I called around to some local historians and a few contacts at the University whose names she and Professor Akembe gave me, and they all promised to look around and let me know what they could find.

Two weeks after I'd met Hank, I called back, but he didn't answer. I called Clare to check on him, and she told me that as far as she knew he was doing fine, so I should just try again.

I felt a little worried anyway, so I called back the next day. Hank answered after several rings.

"Nice to hear from you!" he said. "Really enjoyed your visit. Must be something to psychology after all: I felt a lot better after we talked, and I've been sleeping—*through the night*—since you visited. Haven't done that in sixty years. Say, you should stop back sometime, when you get a chance—I'll bet you're busy with classes now. But if you can make it, I have a few mementos, one thing in particular, that may help you with your story. So you're going to write it up after all? How about that! No one will believe it, you know, and few folks living can attest to it, but I think at last it's a story worth telling. You may be able to find Polly Cooper—she still lives down that way. But I don't know that their town was ever incorporated. You'd have to find Uppsala and walk south and east of there. If nothing else, you'll have a good story to tell your own children. People like stories about—oh, what did they call it back in the 1800s—*local color*! That's it. It's not quite Hamlin Garland's *Main-Travelled Roads*, but it's true, and you're not likely to find anything like it ever again in this world. I'm sure you're a good writer. You should send a copy of your book to my daughter, Brooke, in California—I can send you her address—and to Clare at the diner. I'll bet she'd like to read it."

I told him I was having trouble finding Uppsala on maps or learning anything more about it.

"Oh, I think I heard that, now that you remind me, that the townspeople had changed the name. But I never did hear what they changed it *to*. Been a long time since I was in that town, and we were out of state for so long that I've lost touch with so much—and just think of how much it will have changed, with electricity and all. It's not all that far from here, though, where I live now. It was hard to get to by car then, but roads go everywhere now. I'll bet we could drive to it. Ha! Here I am thinking you have time for that sort of thing. Just call me if you have questions—how's that? And if you're down this way, feel welcome to stop by. Next time I'll order us some of Clare's root soup from the diner. I don't get many visitors now. Not many folks living and healthy enough to travel remember old Hank Peck. Funny: I wasn't so much of a talker in the old days. Maybe age does that to you. You take good care, son."

One Saturday in late October Clare from the diner called me. She had gone to Hank's house to deliver some groceries. He was sitting in his chair on the porch, and the University football game was playing on his radio. But he was dead. She said his face looked calm, even happy: he looked like he was sleeping soundly.

I told her that he was well into his nineties and that he had lived a full life. He had been a good man, a kind man, a brave man: the world doesn't see too many like that in our time.

But I couldn't find the right words to say so that I could help her feel any better. She cried and cried, as if she had lost her own father. To tell you the truth, I cried, too, though I tried not to let Clare know that. It's true: the world doesn't see many Hank Pecks anymore.

I couldn't get there until the next weekend, and they'd already had the funeral service. They had the body cremated, but had a stone set in the nearest cemetery, not too far away. Clare told me Hank's daughter and a few other relatives and friends had come. Polly Cooper had come, but no one had an address or phone number for her. I should contact the Oneida nation and see if they can help me find her. How much she could tell me about Hank's story—and I'll bet she has many stories of her own!

In Hank's house and barn they had found blacksmithing and woodworking materials, gardening implements, some simple, comfortable-looking casual clothes, lots of books and maps, some railroad and automobile memorabilia, and several medals from World War I, including a Victory Medal and a Medal of Honor. No one at the funeral service could remember Hank's ever having shown the medals to anyone. If there had been anything else left of Hank's belongings, family and friends had taken it.

Among his books they found state and US histories, accounts of and novels and poetry about the First World War, books on mining and metalwork and gardening, a bunch of other novels, mostly from the nineteenth century, but with a good selection of American realism and naturalism, a few different translations of the Bible and one New Testament in Greek, some translations of Old English poetry and Icelandic sagas (including *The Saga of the Volsungs* and *Njal's Saga*), and copies of *The Song of Roland*, *The Nibelungenlied*, *El Cid*, and what looked like a first British edition of *The Lord of the Rings*. Somewhere he had turned up early editions of Dickens and Austen.

Clare had asked the family if she could take one of Hank's books to give to me: it was an old hardcover edition of Dickens' *Our Mutual Friend*.

I treasure that book. I never did find out what that particular thing was that he wanted to show me.

Though I had hardly known him, I had a hard time believing that Hank Peck was no longer in the world. He came from a different generation, a time that now seems far, far away, a time when ghosts walked the earth, and, at their best, men and women met them together, face to face, with unclouded minds and honest hearts.

All I can do for Hank now is to write the story he told me as he told it and hope people can still feel about him the way Clare and I do.